Andrey Grodzinskiy

IN THE LOYAL EYES
A THE FRIEND

London 2022

Published by Hertfordshire Press Ltd © 2022
e-mail: publisher@hertfordshirepress.com
www.hertfordshirepress.com

IN THE LOYAL EYES OF A FRIEND

Andrey Grodzinskiy

English

Editor Steven M. Bland
Translator Dana Zheteyeva
Illustrator Yuliya Yevtushenko Ward
Cover idea Nikita Petrachkov and Andrey Grodzinskiy
Typeset Daniel Brown

---

*British Library Catalogue in Publication Data
A catalogue record for this book is available from the British Library
Library of Congress in Publication Data
A catalogue record for this book has been requested*

ISBN: 978-1-913356-50-7

CONTENTS

Chapter One
LIFE BEFORE   *9*

Chapter Two
IN THE LOYAL EYES OF A FRIEND   *41*

Chapter Three
LIFE AFTER   *87*

Eurasian Creative Guild (London), in partnership with Hertfordshire Press (UK), has been holding an annual Open Eurasian Literary Festival & Book Forum since 2012.

The OEBF consist of a competition and an international festival, where we collaborate together with poets, writers, artists, filmmakers and creatives from every profession in Eurasia (and around the world).

A mutuality based on providing opportunities to establish both insightful and meaningful communication within literacy and cultural spaces. As such, the competition is constructed upon universal principles of openness and interactions between all the arts, contributing to its promotion and discovery of new names. Over 10 years of the Open Eurasia contest, more than 30 authors from 15 countries have been published as part of the winning grants. With these aims in mind, the overall purpose of the OEBF – is to draw the attention of readers, as well as specialists, to the achievements of Eurasian creatives.

www.awardslondon.com

Dedicated to my best friend.
Thank you, granny, that you managed to read this!

Happy are not those who have the best things.
Happy is the one who can take the best from what he has.
Sukhacheva Nina Vasilyevna.

Andrey Grodzinskiy

Don't get a dog, my man:
You're not worthy of its snout!
Just go, but remember, my man:
Their death is worse for us than the gallows.

Konstantin Alexeyevich went upstairs to his study on the second floor. He angrily slammed the door, walked to the desk, and took out tobacco, cigarette papers and filters from the upper drawer.

"How do I explain to her… to them why I'm saying 'No'?"

He exhaled in an attempt to calm himself down.

"It's alright for my daughter… but my wife? She's heard this story dozens of times. And still, as soon as Mila strikes up a conversation about a dog, Eve immediately sides with her! Have I not earned some peace?"

He sat in his frayed black armchair where he'd written over a hundred literary works: novels, novellas, short stories… and such a huge amount of poems!

Konstantin Alexeyevich always felt better when he was

writing. Whatever was happening in his life, whatever intrigues were being plotted against him, however vehemently his wife was nagging him, he always knew that as soon as he sat with his manuscript, everything would fall into place.

Drawing his German typewriter near, Konstantin Alexeyevich started working on the first chapter of his new book, when he was interrupted by a faint knock on the door.

He sighed helplessly.

'Please, enter, Mila.'

The door opened, and an eighteen-year-old beauty entered the room, hiding her guilty eyes.

'Dad,' she said.

Konstantin Alexeyevich glanced at his daughter.

"She is grown-up already. It's probably time to tell her why I'm not succumbing to her mum and her urgings."

He moved the typewriter and the manuscript away and placed his smoking accessories in front of him.

'Dad,' the girl repeated; 'do I ask for much? Just to get a little puppy… It's no big deal!'

The father poured a pinch of tobacco onto the paper, placed a filter into it, and folded a cigarette. He got up, went to the shelves containing his works, and took a thin book in a hardcover from them.

Then he motioned to his daughter to sit on the sofa and started reading aloud.

Chapter One
Life before

This story begins in the sunny city of Tashkent.

The evening of the ninth of July was hot as usual. Alexander and his family, consisting of his mother and his father, were spending time in their flat, which was fully equipped with air conditioners.

The heat outside during the day was exhausting. Even a short stay under the summer sun of Uzbekistan made the soles of one's footwear melt.

Sasha[1] was in high spirits, for the next day, on the tenth of July, he would turn eighteen.

He already knew what his parents were going to give him. It was a car! So what if it was not the latest and trend-

---

1   Sasha – diminutive name for Alexander (throughout the book: Sasha, Sash, Sanya)

iest type? It still opened huge landscapes and opportunities for this young man to fulfil his ambitions.

Alexander anticipated the moment when he and his friends from his house - and not only those - would go on a journey to the Charvak Reservoir, where there was always an atmosphere of celebration, and where they would sit in one of the cafés or restaurants and order some kebabs and shurpa[2].

The place where Sasha wanted to go the most in his car was known as "The Barrel". It was an almost kilometre long street crowded with various premises where they served the Uzbek national cuisine. What made it special was the ambience, which made each guest want to stay longer and keep on enjoying the exquisitely delicious food.

Not only was Alexander eagerly awaiting the moment when he would get behind the wheel of his brand-new car, but he was also expecting his friends to be tripping over each other to congratulate him. And Sasha had no doubt that the first one would be his best friend, Denis, who lived nearby.

They had been friends from an early age, even though Den was two years younger than him. A big group of them, all the boys from the C-1 district, would spend all day playing football or hide and seek and were reluctant to go home when someone's mom was the first to call for her kid from the window. And then, the rest of the mothers would start to look out of their windows, as if it was their turn now.

Eighteen-year-olds always have a certain perspective wherever they are and whatever situation they're in. It's the

---

2   Shurpa – a Central Asian dish (a rich lamb and vegetable soup)

age when the life they've already been living surreptitiously becomes more or less legal.

Sometimes, relations with parents change drastically. Each silly delinquency that was allowed to be written off at a young age is now supposed to be discussed with all seriousness, so that the young man or a girl understands that growing up is not only about the moments of bliss they want to fill all their free time with, but is also about the responsibility they need to take on their shoulders and carry as there are no other options.

However, understanding what parents often demand from their children rather than ask for doesn't always come right after the family blamestorming. We are all different. Each of us has our own way, and nobody knows where it will take us in the end.

Alexander woke up at a few minutes past five, jumped off his bed, and checked his phone. As he'd assumed, the first message was from Denis, who was wishing his friend everything a sixteen-year-old could gather in his head.

Sasha smiled. He relished the moments he'd foreseen. Having automatically scanned the rest messages, Alexander replied 'Thanks!' to each of them.

The family gathered for breakfast. Anatoliy Valeryevich gave his son an appraising look and the typical for a strict father squint. His mother was beaming with pride and happiness at such a deeply important moment when her beloved boy had come of age.

His father got up, went to the bedroom for a minute,

and returned with the car keys in his hand.

'Happy birthday, son! Be careful; don't crash it on the first day.'

'Happy birthday, sonny!' his mom uttered. 'We love you so much,' she said, and her eyes brimmed with tears.

'Come on, mom, I'm a grown-up now. Why are you crying?'

'Because children remain children forever - at least for their parents!' Larisa Viktorovna replied, wiping her eyes.

On the evening of the tenth of July, Sasha left the house. His blue jeans, white t-shirt and black loafers shouting out there would be a party soon. He decided not to drive that evening as it would be possible to get to the place, but coming back would be a problem as the guys were going to have a lot to drink.

Denis emerged from the next entrance of the house, approached Alexander, and presented him with his birthday gift in a small, beautiful paper bag.

Sasha opened it immediately.

'Dens, thank you! Is it the cologne I wanted to get myself? You sure know what to get me,' Sasha said, hugging his buddy.

'Of course I do,' Denis pronounced, smiling shyly. 'Spray some of it on now; we're going to a restaurant and then a club. There's a chance we'll hook up with someone there,' he said, laughing and winking at his friend.

'The main thing is not to hook something from those we'll leave the club with,' Sasha noted, smiling sarcastically.

'We should go to a drugstore on the way. I don't want to be looking for protection in the middle of the night like we did last time.'

The party was a blast. The restaurant, which was fairly close to the centre of the city, greeted its guests with loud contemporary music which was driving the young people crazy. There were so many pretty girls in short dresses which hardly covered their enticing bodies...

There were fifteen people at the festive table — ten guys and five youngish girls. The first toast was delivered by Denis, who wished his friend all the best once more.

Having had a fair amount to drink, the group headed for the dance-floor ready for adventures.

'What do you think about the one in the yellow dress?' Aziz asked Sasha. 'Good, isn't she?'

'Indeed. You probably noticed that her gorgeous body ideally balances her plain face,' Alexander shouted, laughing.

The music was so loud it had the ability to devour any conversation.

'Eh? I don't understand what you don't like about her face. I wasn't even going to look at it, anyway. Alright, I'm going there,' Aziz said with a spark in his eyes, and plunged into the dancing throng.

Sasha sat at the table trying to catch his breath after the dance that had just finished and filled his friends' shot glasses with vodka. Everyone came to the table.

'Guys, I'd like to make a toast to you,' he shouted. 'Thank you for being with me today. And we're having so much fun. We're young, so let's party like we're never gonna grow old!' he said, and they clinked glasses.

The vodka, which they'd been drinking lightly in the beginning, now demanded some snacks. Already a bit tired of dancing, the guys and girls were sitting on the chairs trying to communicate.

The guys who'd left their girlfriends home didn't just enter the club, they barged in. They were in a drunken haze and were sure to have a severe hangover in the morning. When did such a trifle ever stop young people, though? Besides, at that age, they had a false perception that such a life was going to last forever.

'What are we going to drink?' asked Rustam. 'Or did you have enough?'

'What are you talking about? Some whiskey!?' Denis suggested.

'Order whatever you want,' Sasha announced with a smug nonchalance. 'I hope at least some of you will recall this night tomorrow,' he concluded ironically.

A litre of whiskey was finished in the blink of an eye, as each of them had only about a hundred grams of it. So when a waiter approached the table, Sasha, who was still able to talk intelligibly — or at least he thought so, ordered two more bottles.

Standing near their house, dead drunk at six in the morning, Denis and Sasha started a conversation. They didn't feel any nostalgia for the past as they belonged to some sort of the elite or "gilded youth," and were looking to the future boldly without a hint of hesitation.

'Did you notice, Dens? Several times we had parties and the two of us stayed up in the end, just like now,' Sasha started. 'How many things are ahead of us we can do? And I want to think that life will lead us together on our way.'

'Dude, you can't even imagine how happy I am that we're friends and have known each other from an early age! Thank you for always covering my ass. How many times have I got into trouble, and how many are still ahead knowing my temper! It's so cool that at such moments I have someone like you. You're the one who'll always come to rescue me. Happy birthday, bro!'

'You know, Den, here I am, sitting on this wooden bench and thinking — it would be so great if everything would stay as it is now. I don't even want to imagine that one day our get-togethers could stop; that each of us would marry and dive into his family life completely. I think in the future we should be able to find time for such a night, at least…' he stopped short and glanced at his watch, 'for morning talks,' Sasha corrected himself.

'Of course, my friend; this isn't even up for discussion! Even when we're married and settled down, we'll still have fun getting into situations that will probably be a little different, but the essence of them will remain the same.'

'Tell me, Dens,' Sasha asked carefully, 'how is it going with Anya? It looks like you're in love with her, right? Otherwise, how could you explain spending so much time with her?'

'Honestly, the hell do I know, Sasha? I'm attracted to her — I can tell that for sure. Her body is perfect — you saw that for yourself. She has a cute, pretty face. Big green eyes...'

'But tell me, are you still seeing other girls and sleeping with them?' Alexander asked, chuckling.

'Naturally!' Denis responded, catching the contagious laughter of his friend. 'You know me! I can't hang out with just one girl. It's not fun.'

'Even if you love her?'

'And what's in it for me with that love!? And Anya doesn't know anything about my exploits.'

'Well, that's not for long,' Sasha responded.

'Oh, come on! How would she find out? Women are dumb in general, though they are beautiful. Anya is no exception. Let it be as it is. What about you and Regina?'

'Everything's stable, no surprises. She's good, but I can feel there's a big gap between us.'

'What do you mean?'

'Well, what I mean is that although we grew up in the same city, we're different mentally. I think it's because of the material situation — it seems like there's an abyss between our families.'

'But that's even easier, bro! This scenario's better than when you're in the pursuing mode.'

'I don't get it.'

'Well, you can give her much more than the majority of people, right? And that means she won't even think about cheating on you or something like that.'

'So, what you want to say is that it's enough to shower her with expensive gifts bought with my parents' money and she'll be mine forever? It's so tawdry and dull.'

'But you love her, no? So, what's the problem? She would get what she wants, and you'd get her. It's a win-win situation!'

'No, it's not like that,' Sasha rebuked his friend, lighting up yet another cigarette. 'If it happens the way you've just described, then I'll always dominate her. Yes, of course, she wouldn't have a choice except to obey me completely, but see what would happen then: I'd get bored. And why do I need such a relationship?'

'Oh, bro, it looks like you don't even know what you want,' Denis replied, laughing aloud.

'Alright, let's get some sleep, I guess,' said Sasha. 'You'll have to listen to another lecture from your parents for coming home drunk in the morning.'

'That's fine. The main thing is to get to my bed and not fall in the corridor like I did last time.'

***

Two years passed. One day in March, Denis called Sasha.

'Hey, how are you? What are you up to today?'

'Hey, I'm about to leave university and wouldn't mind drinking a bottle of beer. What's your plan for today?'

'Hey, that's great. We'll finish our training at Pakhtakor[3] in twenty minutes, and then my little brother and I are go-

3   'Pakhtakor' – an Uzbek professional football club based in Tashkent.

ing to have some beers. Would you like to pick us up and we'll go somewhere together?'

'Who are you going to drink beer with? With your little brother?' Sasha asked, bewildered. 'What brother? And what are you doing at Pakhtakor?'

'His name is Kostya. I told you about him, don't you remember? That's okay; it doesn't matter. Uncle Yasha made me join the tennis group here, so I'm playing now.'

'And how do you like tennis? Especially after the taekwondo and boxing you've been going to for twelve years?' asked Sasha, laughing over the phone.

'What can I say? It's boring... that's why I want to drink. So, will you pick us up?'

'Alright, I'll be there in thirty minutes. You'll finish by then.'

'Cool. Okay, bro, see you soon.'

'See ya.'

With their elbows propped on the car, Denis, Sasha, and Kostya were drinking heavy beer. Konstantin was fifteen years old, and he clearly noticed with what distrust the friend of his so-called brother shook his hand. Kostya had got used to that. From his childhood, he'd only hung out only with older boys as there were no others in his house.

They got a couple of bottles each so they wouldn't have to go again, as they knew one bottle wouldn't be enough.

Sasha decided to take an interest and started a conversation.

'What are you doing in general, Kostya?' he asked.

'I'm studying at a lyceum,' the latter replied modestly.

'What kind of lyceum?'

'He's in the "West"[4],' Denis explained.

'I thought there was just a university there. Fun,' Sasha replied. 'What are you going to do after that?'

'I'm not sure,' Kostya replied honestly. 'For now, I'm planning to enter a program that would allow me to cut down a year and a certain amount of money. I'm in my first year now, so I still have time.'

'Look, you're going to study in the same brainery with Den,' said Sasha, laughing. 'That's fine. It's Friday today, Den. Are we going anywhere tonight?'

'Of course, let's… but where?'

'We'll decide. Kostya, are you with us?'

'No, I doubt I can join you.'

'What's the problem?' Denis asked, quite surprised.

'I promised to help my uncle, which means I'll be busy until late at night. Anyway, guys, thanks for the invitation, but I'll have to decline.'

'It's up to you,' Sasha said indifferently. 'Denis, let's meet up at seven in the yard. We'll decide then.'

'No problem.'

Maybe Konstantin wanted to join them. However, even at his young age, he could already discern if the one doing the inviting was genuine or was simply being polite. There are countless such moments in life, and it would be great if each of us could discern the real desire to communicate or meet a certain person that we encounter.

---

4   'West' - an academic lyceum under the International Westminster University in Tashkent.

When you're young, you want to be the centre of everything that's going on — to arrange parties, meet new people, and show your significance by telling people about your modest successes.

Oh, youth! Probably the best time for the important things which only obtain their significance much later. When we're young, due to lack of experience, our decisions are more emotional than rational. That's where the romanticism is, bound to the nostalgic reminisces of those bewildering parties with their pomposity and absence of any shame which we wanted to go to over and over again. But each stage of life is splendid in its own way, even if it doesn't bring the same satisfaction.

***

Konstantin's mind was completely overwhelmed with thoughts of her. Her name was Angelika. He fell in love with her at first sight and started acting decisively — non-intrusive phone calls in the evenings, bouquets of flowers, congratulations on all possible holidays. As often happens when we're in love, Konstantin put his heart and soul into every deed, not realising that day by day he was growing more distant from the object of his admiration.

Angelika didn't want to give him a single chance. She told him straight: 'I'm sorry, you're a good guy, but I prefer older guys.' Such a transparent statement was a sobering factor for Kostya, though for the next three long years he couldn't forget Angelika and sought her face in every one passing by in the crowd.

***

Den and Sasha met that same evening in front of their house as they'd agreed. They were smoking near Alexander's car when Denis, who'd been trying to hide his disappointment, decided to spill the truth to his friend about the cause of his sombre mood.

'Anya and I split up,' he squeezed out.

'What?' Sasha exclaimed, not believing his ears. 'What happened?'

'Nothing much. Remember when we went to my dad's country house recently? I was there with a girl. I think her name was Katya. To cut a long story short, Anya found out about it.'

'Oh, come on. If she knew about all your exploits, that's when you should worry. But this one is easy. Tell her it was a friend… say, Roma's, though you should warn him first. And that's it. Believe me, I don't think she knows any details. I'm interested in another thing — who ratted you out?'

'It could be Roma himself! I don't know. Listen, what if she's bluffing? I told her I was going there with the guys. Do you think she's just checking up on me?'

'Hmm, even if that's true you can easily say you forgot; she'll believe that a hundred percent. Anya knows that you're able to get drunk like a pig and not remember anything afterward. Listen to me. You have two strategies you can use in this situation. The first one, which is less acceptable, is to buy her an enormous and luxurious bouquet, come to her and say you're sorry, and then Anya will almost certainly forgive you; it's just a matter of time. The other option is to just say you don't remember anything, and even if there were some girls, she still has no reason to be jealous.'

'And why is this second strategy so good?' Den asked, perplexed.

'Because she'll become outraged and start saying she knows everything already and so on, and then you'll say: "We were drinking all night. Sasha and me were steaming in the bathhouse and playing billiards. I didn't care about anyone else as I just wanted to have a heart-to-heart talk with my best friend." After that you'll pause and finish with this: "It's so unpleasant you have such an opinion about me. If you were so sure about me cheating on you, you'd just disappear without any explanation. I know you." And that's it! You win. My advice to you, young man, is to learn how to hide all the traces of your romantic exploits, otherwise you'll lose your Anya forever, and you'll be the biggest idiot I've ever met in my life.'

Everything worked out fine that time. Anya had no evidence. Despite all his efforts to hide his flings, however, Anya and he broke up in the end. And even though he'd expected something like that, Sasha used any opportunity to remind his friend what a stupid mistake he'd made.

***

The flow of time takes us to a few years later when Konstantin had become a good friend to Denis, and Alexander had started to trust the young man who never allowed doubts to creep into his words or actions.

One evening in May, Denis took his mother to the airport and then called his best friends - Alexander, Zhenya, and Kostya - offering them to meet up at his place, where they could drink as much alcohol as possible and generally do whatever they pleased.

And, as usual, when men meet around two o'clock in the morning, a heart-to-heart conversation began.

'Denis, try to understand, even if I don't like Lena, and I haven't been discreet about that from the first day of our acquaintance, I'm not going to do that now. But you do understand that she's not right, whatever one may say! Did you propose to her? Yes. You came to her birthday with a ring, thus making her dream come true, right? Yes, it was just like that. Then why did she, I'm not gonna call her names now, dare to ban you, and, moreover, complain that the ring was without a diamond? What's that about?'

'Kostya,' Sasha started in a calm voice. 'Let them deal with it themselves. That's their business. And tell me, please, what is it about Lena that you don't like? Your sworn brother chose her himself. What's the problem?'

'The thing is that she's not interested in anything but beauty salons and fitness clubs,' Kostya replied with drunken indignation in his voice. 'Tell me, Denis, what did she attract you with? She can't be compared with those girls we're used to seeing you with. Of course, I understand, but I still can't see the thing you found in her.'

'You know, Kostya, you probably wouldn't understand such things yet, but only for now. When you grow up, you'll understand what I'm about to say to you. Lena and I are approximately at the same level of wealth, and it's important to me. I went out with many girls, hung out with them, well, you know it, and each of them wanted me to solve their problems. I'm not against that, but what did they give me? Lena is from a good family; her wonderful parents sur-rounded her with care and material things. Yes, maybe she's not as beautiful in appearance and her temper isn't the best, but I like her and I'll try to fix what I've already done.'

'I get you,' Konstantin replied in a downhearted voice. 'In that case, answer me: do you love her? But you should know that by answering this question you must understand that I don't just mean the passion that Lena evokes in you but the desire and the understanding of a simple fact that you, Denis, are ready to live with her for the rest of your life.'

'Yes, I love her,' Den answered without hesitation.

'Wonderful,' Sasha pronounced calmly. 'Shall we close this topic?'

'No,' Kostya said in a calm voice, too. 'Den, bro, please explain to me why, if you love her so much, do you continue having affairs? What's the reason behind that? If you're say-ing that Lena is so gorgeous and right for you, then why are you cheating on her?'.

'I love living on the edge. When I think that one day she'll find out about my exploits, I think about how I'll try to surround her with such care that any other girl could only dream of! If you wish, such things only motivate me more, and I'd do anything to make my girl and my wife-to-be feel so desired.'

'Yes, Denis,' Konstantin replied sadly. 'I might be younger, but I don't even want to try to understand your point of view, and as for accepting it — it's out of the question. I told you I can draw realistic conclusions based on the situations that happen to me or my friends. So, you can act as you think is right, and I'll wish you happiness, sincerely, only you should know my opinion…'

'No,' Alexander interrupted him. 'Enough. Please, keep your opinion to yourself. We came here with one goal — to get hammered. As for me, this goal hasn't been achieved yet.'

He got a glass of vodka.

'Let's drink to each of us obtaining our slice of happiness, whatever it costs us.'

The evening smoothly flew into the deep of night, and for Kostya, it was time to go. He had to return home where his family was waiting for him and worrying about him, as they knew how such get-togethers with Den and the guys usually ended.

He walked along a straight path between the houses in sheer silence and solitude. The latter was gambling with him, and that game could have an acceptable ending, whoever was right among them.

There were a lot of temptations in Konstantin's life —

pretty girls who were ready to give themselves up on the first date, affordable alcohol he treated himself to now and then, and the desire to give everything up and just leave — that was the alluring thing which was playing on his mind more than anything else.

That period in Alexander's, Denis's and Konstantin's lives could be characterised as a great mutual pastime that was imprinted in each of their minds. They kept on communicating and seeing each other.

Eventually, the noisy parties would be replaced by warm-hearted gatherings, pompous restaurants and cosy little places where they wouldn't be bothered, and their desire to better themselves would turn into a humane understanding of this or that situation. It could have gone on like that, like a gradual ascent to a certain peak. However, the dialogue had already taken place for the umpteenth time precisely at the moment when it seemed that the three of them had been standing in one place for too long.

'I'm leaving, Kostya,' Denis said with chagrin in his voice.

'Where? When?' Konstantin asked in bewilderment.

'To the States. My stepbrother lives there with his family. I'll crash at his place first, then rent something.'

'Why so suddenly? I didn't see that coming.'

'Yeah, I only told Sasha about it, and now I'm telling you.'

'Is it connected with Lena somehow?'

'Partially.'

'But she's pregnant! She's going to have your baby. Will

you leave your kid without a father?'

'But do they need me?' Denis asked, raising his eyes full of sincerity. 'Every member of her family made me realise we're never going to be together.'

'So what? Are you going to give up just like that?'

'There's another reason too.'

'I can guess what that is. It's the business that you start- ed with Hurshid, right? Is it so bad?'

'Okay, look, the situation is the following — it's either I am leaving on a visitor visa, which I already have in my hands, or I'm going to prison as the director of our company under the articles on economic crime. I am not keen on going behind bars, especially as I wouldn't be able to help Lena or our future child from there for sure.'

'Does she know about that?'

'Of course not,' Den pronounced, smiling sadly.

'You didn't tell her?'

'Why would I? Even if I wanted to do, she and all her family are totally ignoring me. I don't have a choice.'

'What about your mom? Grandmother?'

'I'll find a job and send money to my mother. We'll wait until my father solves his problems in Russia, and then everything will be cool, believe me.'

'Have you bought tickets yet?'

'Yeah; I'm leaving on August fifteenth. Will you see me off, Kostya?' Denis asked with hope in his voice.

'What kind of silly question is that? Of course, I'll see you off. But it's like in ten days…'

'Exactly. We're going for drinks at the "Finland" on Saturday. What about you? Will you join us? Will you see the old man off with beer and women of easy virtue?'

'Do I have a choice, really?' Kostya answered, laughing, though this chuckle of his was more nervous than from the heart.

Konstantin was now alone. Who would be left to tell badass stories while drinking a glass of cognac?

"Yeah…" Kostya thought, "after August the fifteenth this place will be vacant forever."

That last night Konstantin remembered for the rest of his life. The four of them were sitting on the patio at the "Finland" café where Zhenya[5]'s father was the owner, drinking tap beer that was still tasty then. They were snacking on pork kebabs and discussing what would happen after the departure of their mutual friend.

Kostya didn't know that Denis had borrowed quite a lot of money from Zhenya for his business and hadn't returned it. He'd done the same with Sasha, though in his case the sum was significantly smaller.

'So, bro, let's raise this toast to you that everything goes fine in the new place,' Alexander spoke.

'Thank you, dear friend,' Denis replied.

'Den, have you found a place to work in the States?' Kostya asked.

'Well, my brother has two car washes there, and, as you might know, it's quite a profitable business in America; even better than here. I'll start there and look for something more worthwhile at the same time.'

---

5   Zhenya – diminutive name for Evgeniy (throughout the book – Zhenya, Zhenyek, Evgeniy)

'I can imagine what kind of girls you'll have there,' Zhenya interjected. 'I've seen pictures on social media… You'll have something to hunt for!'

'Denis just needs a certain level of alcohol in his blood, and then he'll drag anything that moves into his bed,' Sasha said, laughing sonorously.

'And whatever doesn't move, he'll move himself!' Kostya backed him up.

Everybody laughed and clinked their glasses filled with beer, and then they all fell silent for some time, each of them lost in their own thoughts.

Zhenya was ruminating on how lucky Denis was and what opportunities were opening up for him in the United States, especially in New York, where his brother lived. Kostya was trying to draw a picture of the future in his head, where there was no sworn brother of his there. And looking at his closest friends, Denis realised that his decision about leaving was all too spontaneous and ill-considered, though he also understood there was no other option after what he'd done in Tashkent.

Alexander, who looked even more pensive than the others, sank deeper and deeper with the only thought in his mind — his best and truest friend who he'd known from an early age, who he'd covered for and helped out in all sorts of unimaginable situations, who was like a little brother from another mother — it was him, and not anybody else who was spending his last night in his hometown. Sasha was trying to scold himself for overlooking Denis, for not controlling him enough. Only a few years later would the realisation dawn on him that he couldn't have done anything to change it. All those things happened the way they were supposed to.

'So, guys, shall we ask for a bill?' Sasha said. 'It's time to play around with girls.'

'It's on the house today,' Zhenya said modestly. 'I talked to dad, and he said we don't have to pay for anything.'

'Dude, you're the man, Zhenyek!' Denis exclaimed. 'Thank you from the bottom of my heart!'

'That's the spirit,' Sasha said, leaning back in the rattan chair.

'Thank you, Zhenya,' said Kostya.

And thanking the owner of the café, the four friends came out onto the road.

'Shall we get a taxi?' Denis asked.

'Yes, of course. Or did you decide to drive drunk before leaving?' Sasha said with a hint of sarcasm in his voice.

'You think I wouldn't dare to?' Denis asked testily, warm with alcohol.

'And where are we going?' Konstantin quickly chirped, trying to cut the tension.

'To look for the ladies with low levels of social responsibility,' Zhenya said drily.

Denis and Alexander stared at him for a moment, and then guffawed with all their might.

'And where are we going to take them?' Kostya asked in surprise.

'To Zhenya's apartment. He lives alone anyway,' Sasha replied, calming down.

'In that case, let's drop by my house first,' Konstantin

suggested. 'I'll grab some excellent whiskey so we have something to drink just in case. Is that okay?'

'Let's go right now!' Denis commanded enthusiastically.

The clique of fairly drunk young men got the first taxi right away. They were ready for anything the night could offer them.

Sasha, who was the tallest among them, sat in the front seat. Mumbling something petulantly into his beard, Denis opened the back door and sat on the right-hand side. Zhenya sat in the middle, and Kostya, waiting for everyone to settle down, stood and inhaled the sweet air of the Tashkent summer before getting in and slamming the door.

The atmosphere at the spot to meet girls of easy virtue was vibrant — the majority of young men surreptitiously came up to women of a certain age and inquired what kind of girls were available and what the price was for the night. The four friends did the same. It took about an hour before they finally agreed with two girls who seemed quite good-looking in the pitch dark to join them. Only on the way to Zhenya's house, Kostya and Sasha, seeing the faces of the girls, were horrified by the choice that Denis had taken the liberty of making; but the fun was just getting started.

Arriving at Zhenya's, the group of six, all trying to appear inconspicuous, went up to the ninth floor of an apartment building. Zhenya would later say: 'Thank God we didn't run into anyone that evening. How terrible those prostitutes were!'

Sasha and Kostya preferred a relaxing massage to sex, but Denis and Zhenya didn't leave the bedroom for a long time. Having received their massage, Sasha and Kostya sat down in the living room in front of the TV and poured a little whiskey into their glasses. After clinking glasses and drinking to the luck of their friend who was leaving them, they decided it would be nice to play football on the Play-Station.

In the morning at around seven or eight when Denis and Zhenya were peacefully sleeping in the other room, Alexander and Konstantin, having paid and seen off the girls, looked at each other with tired eyes and decided it was time to go home. Saying goodbye to their sleepy friends, they went outside.

'Listen, would you like to get to a café nearby? They're open 24/7,' suggested Sasha.

'Are you hungry already?'

'To tell the truth, I'm so hungry it's as if it wasn't me who ate half a kilo of pork kebabs a few hours ago. What about you?'

'Actually, I am hungry too. I just didn't want to mention it as we're obviously both exhausted.'

'That's alright,' Sasha replied. 'We'll get a taxi. It's a three-minute ride!'

'Excellent!' Kostya chimed in joyfully. 'It's high time to have breakfast.'

***

The day of the departure arrived, and Denis called Kostya.

'Hey, bro; how are you? Are you sleeping?'

'Hey; of course not. When should I come?'

'Come by eleven.'

'Isn't it too early?'

'Just in time. We just wanted to have some beer with Sanya. What about you, do you mind?'

'Got it; I'll be there at eleven.' Kostya responded.

At the designated time, Konstantin's car pulled up beneath the windows of the house where Denis and Sasha lived. Alexander came out first.

'Hey, college boy, how are you?' he asked drowsily.

'What's up, Sanya? All okay, and you?'

'How should I feel when my best friend is leaving?'

Kostya didn't know what to say.

Sasha lit a cigarette and was anxiously pacing while waiting for Denis. The latter came out of the house, and the entrance door slammed loudly.

They drove to the first convenience store three hundred metres from their meeting point, and Denis and Alexander got out of the car to buy a couple of beers.

'Well, guys, thank you,' Denis began heartily. 'We had a lot of funny moments,' he said, looking at Sasha, 'though there were sad ones, too' he added, turning his gaze to Kostya.

'Thank you so much, guys! I feel your support… I know how I'll miss that in the States.'

'That's alright, Dens, we'll survive. We don't live in prehistoric times. Come on, we'll call each other. Just don't get lost, you know, otherwise, I know you,' Sasha warned with his index finger. 'Look at me! I can find you anywhere, Dens!'

'What are you talking about, bro? How can I get lost? I'll be dying of boredom there!'

'Guys,' Kostya said. 'It's time to go, otherwise you'll miss your flight, Den.'

'You're right,' Denis agreed, looking at his watch. 'May I finish my beer in your car?'

'Of course; just don't spill it,' Kostya pronounced, smiling.

They all sat down, and the car took off.

Tashkent airport was awash with evening lights. It was a mesmerising sight — planes were taking off and landing in spite of the natural change of day and night. How many longed-for encounters did each flight contain? A son who hadn't seen his parents for several years; a girl who'd kept her vow to be faithful to her beloved man; a guy who'd lived through the last months only for the sake of the moment when he saw the eyes of his friends once again. But at the same time, their souls were pierced with worries about bidding farewell.

Sometimes, there was a feeling that a man about to depart was not only leaving his hometown. It felt like he was slipping out without saying a word, without saying goodbye, from your life. That was the exact feeling that Kostya had when he hugged his sworn brother for the last time.

'Denis,' he said once they stopped embracing each other. 'You write to me. Don't disappear on me, please. Have a safe flight!'

'Of course, I'll write. Life doesn't end here,' Den replied, smiling.

'Alright, bro,' Sasha said, and hugged his friend. 'I hope things go better for you there than here.'

Konstantin and Alexander stood at the security station near the departure gate and watched the one who'd made them meet go further and further without any promise to return.

On the way home, Kostya, driving the car in his usual very careful manner, was absorbed in his thoughts. His so-called brother had gone, and it felt like his life was now divided into several parts.

Alexander didn't break the silence that reigned in the car. He was ruminating on what to do following his best friend's departure. And he could be gone forever.

'What do you think, Sash? Will he ever come back?' Kostya suddenly asked.

'Of course he will,' Alexander replied confidently. 'Only I don't know when it that will be.'

'Well, we'll wait for him for a pilau[6],' Kostya attempted to jest.

Sasha turned away with a very sad look on his face and stared out the window. They didn't speak again during the entire journey.

The car turned into the lane he'd known since child-hood. Alexander got out and took out his cigarettes and a lighter.

---

6   Pilau – Uzbek national dish (stewed meat with rice and vegeta-bles)

'Alright, Kostya, I'm gonna head. Thanks for the lift.'

'It's fine. See you.'

Sasha approached his porch and glanced at Denis's windows. There was light on in them.

"It's probably Aunt Vika waiting for her son's flight to depart," he thought. "Then she'll go to bed after that."

Alexander threw away the cigarette butt and went to his floor. He opened the door, and it suddenly dawned on him — it had been so great to have a friend who lived in the same house! They could text or call each other, invite each other over, meet up and have a beer.

"Yeah… there won't be any such opportunities anymore."

***

Kostya arrived home and went on with his life. University and the gym occupied most of his time. Taking care of his family, which he even grew a little closer to, brought him pleasure. He often thought about his sworn brother, who felt something like a reminisce extremely distant from the present.

The only person from their crowd who was truly happy about what had happened was Sasha's girlfriend. Although Ilona pretended to share her boyfriend's rueful feelings, in reality, she was celebrating Den's departure as a victory.

They'd been dating for over a year at that time, and had started living together. This brought tangible changes to Sasha's life. One thing that didn't change, though, was that every time he went outside for a smoke, he called Denis and asked him to meet, which quite often only came to an end in the early morning, so Ilona had to sleep alone. Naturally, such a state of affairs didn't please her at all and led to some minor domestic conflicts.

Ilona and Denis had been bitter rivals from the moment Sasha asked the girl to date. It was difficult, of course, to keep up good relations with his best friend, who was hanging out with various women. And besides, he already had a girlfriend who was practically his wife.

Ilona was outraged by Denis's behaviour. Thinking that Sasha was doing the same, she often threw temper tantrums when the guys made plans to go somewhere.

Alexander took Den's departure hard. Ilona tried to support him and persuade him that she could become at least as good a friend, or maybe even better.

'Why are you grieving Den's departure so much?' Ilona would start yet another quarrel.

'You wouldn't understand. I've known him since my childhood. Do you have such friends? No. I know you don't.'

'So what? I think you're overreacting. Let's stop drinking, or at least just do it on the weekends like we used to.'

'I'll do as I see fit!' Sasha snapped.

'You mean you think it's alright to get hammered every day?' the girl started screaming.

'I drink two or three bottles of beer — that's not getting "hammered." It's how I relax after work. Why are you pestering me?'

'Maybe you miss your exploits, huh?' Ilona asked with an acid tongue.

'What exploits?'

'You know what exploits: you and Den getting prostitutes, or do you think I'm blind? Or maybe dumb?'

'Do you have proof that I cheated on you?' Sasha asked coldly. 'That's what I thought. You don't have any. And I don't see the point in explaining something that never happened.'

'Right, so Denis was getting prostitutes, and you were just standing to one side and smoking. Is that right?' she shouted.

'You could say that. In fact, he sometimes called me when he got a girl in a taxi and didn't know where to take her. A couple of times I gave him keys to the apartment at TTP[7]. Sometimes, Denis didn't even have the strength for that — he was so drunk. I didn't participate when he was with a girl, but as a friend I always tried to help him.'

'You helped him too much! And what did he do for you? Remember when he decided to sell his share in the shop and you gave him the money straight away? And he borrowed money from you and never paid back anything.'

'I told you, he'll send it via money transfer from the States.'

'Are you serious?' Ilona asked sceptically.

'Yes, I believe him.'

A couple of months had passed since Denis left. Returning from the office, out of habit, Sasha went to the

---

7   TTP – is a well-known name for the part of Mirzo-Ulugbek district of Tashkent, where in 1942 the Tashkent Tractor Plant was located.

store. Taking two bottles of beer, he paid at the checkout and left. Having parked the car in front of the house where his parents lived, Alexander sat on the bench where until recently he'd while away the evenings with Denis.

His faith in friendship had evaporated. He'd never thought that his friend could dissolve as if he'd never even exist, and be replaced by a mundane void.

"Communication over the internet will never be able to replace reality," he thought.

Finishing the second bottle, he knew he needed to go home, or rather to the apartment on the ground floor of the nine-storey building which he rented for Ilona and himself. On the one hand, he wanted to spend all his time with this girl, but on the other, every day he became more convinced he needed a friend.

No, he didn't want to deal with people anymore – his past experience spoke against it. What then? Sasha didn't know the answer to this question.

'Why are you so late?' Ilona demanded as he opened the door.

'I was at the office. We were discussing things with dad. Have you cooked anything, or shall we order delivery?'

'No, no need to order anything. Dinner is on the table. Wash your hands, and we'll eat.'

The pasta she had made was delicious.

For some time, Sasha had seemed to be distracted by thoughts about his friend. It was difficult for him to stop drinking every day and being outside more where the air was fresh. He couldn't even remember the last time when

Ilona and he had gone out anywhere together.

"Maybe that's the reason we argue so much," Sasha thought to himself.

Ilona gave the young man a long, sullen look and then decided to interrupt his flow of thoughts.

'Sash, I was thinking… maybe I'm too demanding and actually didn't want to understand you. Denis has left. Just admit it! He's not dead. He's fine; just be happy for him!'

'I'm glad he's in America, but who'll be my friend now?'

'I wanted to talk to you about that. Let's get a dog. There's no better friend than a dog.'

'A dog is a great responsibility. Do you understand that?'

'Alexander,' Ilona uttered determinedly. 'We love each other, and we're going to get married. I think that before we have a child, it would make sense to get a nice dog to take care of.'

'I don't know,' Sasha said wistfully. 'I need to think it over. What breed would you like to have?'

'I don't care,' Ilona said, shrugging her shoulders. 'It's up to you.'

CHAPTER TWO

IN THE LOYAL EYES OF A FRIEND

Sasha woke up at around ten in the morning and wanted to go to work, to his clothing store at once. After lunch, a meeting was scheduled with his father where they were going to discuss the current state of affairs in their family business. Sasha's father got up at six o'clock sharp every morning and was already at the office by eight. This was a habit which had been formed a long time ago, and it wouldn't be possible to change it now.

Mother had cooked breakfast and called her son to the table. Sasha decided that half an hour wouldn't change anything, and with a sad face he came to the table, sat down and stared out the window.

'So, how are you doing?' Larisa Viktorovna asked, looking into her son's eyes.

'It's alright, mum. Everything is fine,' Sasha answered, sighing heavily.

'I can see that you're lying! Why are things like this with you? Does Ilona not want to put up with you?'

'I don't know what she wants,' Alexander said irritably. 'Let her do whatever she wants.'

'Why are you talking like that? You love her, don't you? So what's the problem, then? Go to her place and make peace!'

Sasha just shook his head, but his mother wasn't about to give up.

'What happened between you two?' she continued in a calm voice.

'Nothing special. We were talking about if it would be cool to get a dog, and I said I needed to think it over, to weigh it up. Two months have passed since then, and do you know what she said to me in the end? "You don't wanna get a dog because you're not serious about me"… and then many other words were spoken…'

'And you didn't want to get a puppy?' Larisa Viktorovna asked, surprised. 'I thought you loved dogs.'

'That's not the point, mum. It's the responsibility; don't you understand?'

'Well, that's great! You'll have a reason to go for a walk outside twice a day, or maybe even more often. You're not so keen on going for a walk by yourself, and besides, you won't have a choice.'

'Mum, do you realise that if I get a dog it'll live here in this apartment with you?'

'Why?'

'Because we leave for work in the morning and don't get home until evening. That means there are only two options here — either it lives here with you or one of us has to quit our job, and neither Ilona nor I are ready to do that.'

'I get it, son. But if you don't mind, I'd like to express my opinion — I'd be happy to help. Besides, you know how much I love animals.'

'Thank you, mum,' Sasha said, smiling sincerely, 'but what about dad? Do you think he'll agree so easily?'

'You go and get a dog right now and take it straight to Ilona. You'll see that you'll reconcile at once! Then bring the puppy home and I'll do the talking with your dad. Don't worry about that!'

'Ok, mum. I'll do that.'

'And what breed would you like to get? Have you thought about that?'

'Yes, like a month ago.'

'And what should I wait in a few hours?' Larisa Viktor-ovna asked, smirking.

'An Akita Inu.'

'And what kind of dog is that?' his mum asked. 'I've never heard of it.'

'Do you remember the movie *Hachiko*? That's the dog.'

'Really? That's wonderful! Come on now then, don't waste your time chatting. Go right now!'

'I think you want that dog more than Ilona,' Sasha said ironically.

'Look who's talking!' Larisa Viktorovna replied, laughing. 'Go, son, and don't return without Ilona and the dog!'

A month ago, when reading the descriptions of various breeds, Alexander had been fascinated by Akita Inu.

'It's the closest relative to a wolf. The most faithful and loyal,' it was said. Sasha understood at once — if he were ever to get a dog, it would be only this breed.

"A best friend," he thought to himself. "That's what I need. Who knows, maybe due to certain circumstances I won't even marry Ilona, but at least I'll have a friend who won't betray me or leave.'

Exiting the house, Alexander called the breeder, who informed him that she had three puppies at the moment, two males and one female.

'Anastacia, I'm sorry for the haste, but could I come within half an hour and have a look? If everything is alright, I'll take a puppy at once. Is that okay? Do you mind?'

'No, of course not; please, come. I'll wait for you. I'll send you the address now.'

Having turned into an unfamiliar lane which was quite far from the main street, Sasha got out of the car, lit a cigarette, and looked around. He needed to find a one-storey house with a brown roof, which he spotted without a problem. However, it felt like something inside him was churning, as if what he was about to do would change his life.

Having smoked three cigarettes in a row, he gathered his thoughts, went to the gate and pressed the button on the slightly yellowed intercom.

'Who's there?' said a familiar female voice on the receiver.

'It's Sasha. We talked half an hour ago.'

'Just a minute; I'll come and open the door for you.'

A small door in the gate opened, and Sasha saw a woman of around forty to forty-five dressed in jeans and a man's shirt with long sleeves.

'Come on in, Sasha. Nice to meet you,' said Anastacia.

'Good afternoon; nice to meet you too.'

They went inside, where Sasha's attention was immediately arrested by a fragrant garden surrounded by a metal mesh.

'You have a wonderful garden,' he commented. 'And the net is protection from your pets, right?'

'Thank you, Sasha. Yes. They can be pesky buggers! Have you made up your mind on which you'd like to take, a boy or a girl?'

'I'd like to look first. I think I'll know for sure after that.'

'Well, okay,' Nastya[8] said, smiling as she opened the door. 'Please, go into the house.'

The puppies' mother was locked in a separate room. Sasha heard her barking the moment he crossed the threshold.

Then he discerned a whimper and grumpy yelp that made his heart skip a beat for a second, for he realised he'd be taking that particular puppy home that day. The puppies were kept in a small crate in the living room. On entering the room, Alexander saw them and turned to the baby girl that had just been yelping.

'What's her name?' Sasha asked, without turning his eyes away from the fluffy miracle.

'It's Yoko,' Nastya replied, delighted.

---

8   Nastya – diminutive form of the name Anastacia.

'Does it mean anything in Japanese?'

'Yes, it's "child of the sun."'

'Oh, you are my sunny child!' said Sasha, beaming with happiness. 'Now you'll have a house.'

For the next half an hour, Sasha listened impatiently to the instructions, remembering what to do with the puppy: how to feed her, how many times to walk her, and when to take her to the vet. Having settled all the formalities, he carefully placed the puppy on the front seat of his car and drove off towards his other beloved girl.

'And why have you come here?' Ilona asked irritably as she left her parents' house in the suburbs of the city.

'I want you to come back to me,' Sasha said softly.

'What's the point? Everything will be exactly the same as it was before! I don't want that. You're not serious about me. You make decisions as you see fit without thinking about me, so just keep doing what you want, but this time, without me.'

'I didn't come here alone today,' Sasha said guiltily. 'We both want you to come back.'

'What? Who are you talking about? I didn't see anybody there. Is it Zhenya? You asked him to hide, right? Why is he here anyway?' Ilona asked angrily.

'Ilonchik, take it easy, please. Don't be mad.'

'Why did you come, Sasha?' she inquired, looking into his eyes with a serious expression.

'Let's go to the car and I'll introduce you,' he answered calmly.

Alexander cautiously opened the door and bent down

to pick up Yoko, who was sitting lost in an unfamiliar environment.

'Please meet Ilona, my girlfriend, Yoko, and this is Yoko, the "child of the sun," Ilona.'

Ilona's eyes were brimming with tears. She looked disconcertedly in turns at the young man and the cute white and orange piece of happiness that was struggling to settle down in his arms.

'Wuff-wuff!' Yoko yipped indignantly.

'Ilona, would you like to hold her?'

'Of course,' the girl replied through her tears. 'She's so pretty! What breed is she? It's *Hachiko*, right?'

'Ilonchik, *Hachiko* is the name of the movie, and the breed is Akita Inu.'

The girl took the sweet thing in her arms, which was not used to such excessive attention and was striving to escape. Ilona was patting the puppy with an unspeakably endearing expression on her face that was lit with happiness when she glanced at Sasha as if he were a hero from a fairy tale who had overcome all sorts of obstacles to get to his princess.

'Will you come back to me, Ilona?' Sasha asked uncertainly. 'I can't do without you now — just look how fidgety she is. Let's take care of her together. What do you say?'

Ilona slowly came up and embraced her brave knight. This embrace told him much more than any words that could have been spoken. All three of them were equally happy.

'But how are we gonna take care of her?' Ilona suddenly asked, and, letting Yoko go for a walk, she sat on the old swings near her house. 'We're both working. Will we leave her at home alone?'

'That's what I was trying to tell you when you left me! But don't worry; I've solved that problem, too.'

'Really?' the girl asked disbelievingly. 'And how?'

'Mum agreed to have Yoko living with them. I dread to even imagine her reaction when I bring this miracle home.'

'Oh, that's brilliant! Your mother is a wonderful person!' Ilona said joyfully. 'Wait, though, how does your father feel about it?'

'Mum gave her word she would persuade him. She can - believe me. So, it's not a problem either.'

'Sasha,' Ilona started in a flirtatious tone. 'I'd like to spend tonight in our flat. Let's get some wine, and I'll cook meat. Will you pick me up around nine o'clock? I think I'll be ready by then.'

They kissed on the lips and Ilona went back towards her parents' home, turning around several times as if to make sure that all this was not a vision.

Sasha placed the hungry Yoko on the same seat and, merrily whistling, drove home.

Larisa Viktorovna had, as promised, talked to Anatoly Valerievich, who, it should be mentioned, was not against the fact there would be a dog in the house. Despite his frosty exterior, Sasha's father was fond of animals.

'Well, alright, I agree,' he'd said. 'What breed is he going to get?'

'Some Japanese, like in the *Hachiko* film,' Larisa Viktorovna answered joyfully.

'You don't remember the name?'

'No. It's something in Japanese - I forgot already.'

The entrance door slammed, and Sasha, carefully carrying Yoko in his arms, was slowly ascending the stairs. He had only one thing in mind — he needed to do everything before nine.

'So?' his father asked from the threshold. 'Will you introduce us?'

'This is Yoko — the "child of the sun."'

'Well, the dog is very beautiful indeed.'

'So, where is it?' Larisa Viktorovna asked, running out to the entrance hall. 'Oh, so sweet! Have you chosen a name yet?'

'She has one already. Her name is Yoko.'

'Oh wow! That's a real Japanese name. Is it their tradition to name the puppies at once?'

'As far as I understand, yes. It would have been weird if such a dog was called Alpha or something like that. Only Japanese names suit them.'

'Yes, son. Now you'll get up at six just like me,' his father said with a hint of sarcasm.

'And why's that?' Sasha wondered.

'You think that as she's so small it will be enough to walk her just twice a day? No… You'll take her out five or six times a day.'

'Why so often?' his mother asked.

'Because you'll feed her approximately as often, too,' Anatoly Valerievich smirked.

'Okay, we'll deal with it somehow,' Larisa Viktorovna

said determinedly, 'won't we, Sasha?'

'There's no choice now. I'm not taking her back,' Sasha said, picking up the little dog, which was looking around at a loss. 'By the way, Ilona and I reconciled, so we have a date tonight at nine.'

'Great! Of course, you go. Just tell me what I should feed this beauty,' said his mother, gazing at Yoko with endearment.

'Alright, listen — we'll feed her boiled beef and boiled rice; she can eat that as she's three months old already. Also, we can give her various veggies, like tomatoes or broccoli, but within reasonable limits, of course.'

'Wow!' Anatoly Valerievich exclaimed. 'This dog is going to be better nourished than the majority of the population of our country.'

'Dad, look, as soon as she turns one year old we can actually transfer her to dry food. But as far as I know, such food will cost as much as regular food.'

'I'm not complaining,' his father said. 'I'm just noting that before you disappear in the evening to your beloved one, go to the supermarket and buy some products. Then go to the pet store and get a collar and a leash there.'

'Can it wait until tomorrow?' Larisa Viktorovna interjected.

'No, it can't,' Anatoly Valerievich cut her off. 'And before you go, you'll take Yoko for a walk, Alexander. Do you understand me? Or do you want to make us take on all your responsibilities right away? As they say, if you dance, you must pay the fiddler. And don't forget to buy a liquid-absorbing mat just in case. It's still a baby, and doesn't understand where it can go and where it can't. Also, you won't bring up the dog by yourself; I know that. You should find a trainer. Do you have any in mind?'

'Yeah, I think so,' Sasha replied, scratching the back of his head. 'Our neighbour Kamilla has an acquaintance who lives in the nine-storey block next to us. He's into that kind of thing. I'll get their contact details from Kamilla or Aunt Lola.'

'Great,' his father concluded. 'Well, then don't waste your time, otherwise you won't be able to get everything done. Get your rear in gear!'

***

From the day Sasha brought Yoko home, his life started again as if from the beginning. He was absolutely indifferent to what was going on with his friends, whom he stopped calling. All he needed and what was important to him was right in front of him. The puppy demanded attention — five to six walks a day turned out to be quite a task. Sasha had to accept the fact that taking care of that ginger and white ball of fluff was now an indisputable truth.

A year passed. Yoko grew up and became quite poised, even dignified. One evening when Sasha was walking her, some whim made him think to call Zhenya.

'Zhenyek, hi! How are you? What's new with you?'

'Hey, Sash. I'm doing okay; making minor refurbishments to my apartment. What's with you? I think we haven't talked for about a year, right?'

'Yeah, it feels like it,' Alexander uttered in a guilty voice. 'What are you doing now?'

'Resting. I've been pasting wallpaper for half of the day. Just cooked dinner, now I'm going to eat and then stretch horizontally. Why?'

'I'm having a walk with Yoko here. I thought if you like, maybe you could join us.'

'Have you got a dog? I didn't know. Congratulations! Sounds like a Japanese breed based on the name. Akita Inu?'

'Yep, exactly. So, will you come out with us?'

'Alright; I'll eat quickly.'

'Don't be in a hurry. We'll walk for twenty minutes, Yoko will do her business, and then I'll put her in my car and we'll come to your place. By that time, you'll be finished eating and all that stuff. Okay?

'Okay, I'll wait for you.'

In thirty minutes, Sasha was standing near Zhenya's house, smoking and holding Yoko on the leash. She was looking around with curiosity, as it was her first time in that area. There were so many new smells in the air and the dog was stretching the leash now and then, which made Sasha jerk and hold his cigarette tighter. As he was about to throw the cigarette butt into a nearby bin, Alexander noticed a familiar silhouette in the twilight.

'Hello, worker, how are the repairs going?'

'It's okay. Sick and tired of it, to be honest; seems like there's no end in sight. I thought I'd finish it within a month, and it's the second month now. And only one room is ready, and that's not even completely ready. All the other rooms are a nightmare — all upside down with building materials everywhere.'

The dog was sniffing the new person with interest. Then she made a couple of steps towards him as if inviting him to stroke her.

'Let me introduce Yoko, Zhenya,' Sasha said, loosening the leash.

'Beautiful,' Zhenya noted, scratching Yoko behind the ear. 'And why did you decide to get a dog?'

'Well, Zhenya, that story needs at least a roof above our heads and a bottle of something strong to drink.'

'Only don't say that you broke up with Ilona…'

'Okay, I won't tell that. Would it change anything?'

'Hmm… yeah, I was so glad you called. And when I heard the name of your dog, it filled me with enthusiasm. I was hoping that everything was fine with you, and it turns out it's you who needs to be saved.'

'I already have someone to save me,' Sasha said sadly.

He looked at Yoko, who loyally looked back at her owner.

'Let's go for a little walk. Will you go with me after? I'll leave Yoko at home, and then I'll come back to you. I'll also get a bottle from the bar. What will you drink'

'I don't care. Vodka would be fine; or beer.'

'No, I'm not so standard in my choices – I'm thinking whiskey. Do you mind?'

'I don't. Whiskey, if you say so.'

Autumn weather is rich with inevitable changes that happen day upon day; however, they are often unnoticed by the average citizen. Making certain plans in our heads, we firmly believe in their unfailing realisation, sometimes forgetting that this or that outcome not always depends solely upon us. Circumstances are subject to outside influence, and so much so that only a fool would believe it's only through his efforts that the Earth is still spinning.

Having these walks every day along the streets of Tashkent, Sasha thought a lot about the many things going on in his life. He was devastated that the girl who'd made him decide to break off his previous long-term relationship, who became his favourite, who forced him to get a dog, had left him simply because she said she wanted 'something more.' It was all weird, and it ended quite unpleasantly. The sediment which settled in the bottom of Sasha's soul was impossible to pour out in a conversation or romantic episodes with random girls. No, that parasite dug in deep and plunged its tentacles into his mind that Alexander was vainly trying to cleanse of empty and hopeless thoughts.

The biggest mistake or the grossest assumption a man in a relationship can make is thinking he knows his beloved completely, and she cannot surprise him anymore. This is impossible, however, as not every person is able to fully understand themselves, let alone others.

Watching how agilely Yoko was running next to him wagging her tail, Sasha thought about the concourse of circumstances he found himself in. What if Ilona had persuaded him to get a dog, subconsciously knowing she would leave him? And Yoko would remain the best and the only friend that would never betray him.

The walk was about to end. Stopping at the entrance to the parking lot, Sasha and Zhenya discussed what they should take as a snack to accompany the whiskey.

'Maybe we should go and get a couple of sticks of kebab on the way back?' Alexander suggested.

'Sash, I'm quite low on cash. I dumped all I have into the building materials, and I don't have any other source of income. Asking mum to send me more money wouldn't look good. She's not obliged to, after all. It's my fault that I trusted Den with that money.'

'It's not a problem. Let's drive to the kebab place. Don't worry, buddy, it could happen to anyone.'

'Thanks, Sasha.'

'Why are you thanking me? Stop, I'm begging you!'

Zhenya got out of the car and leaned on it, watching his friend with his dog ascending the stairs to the metal door of his house.

He was thinking about Denis, who had acted so badly towards him. He borrowed a huge amount of money to develop his business and constantly promised jam tomorrow. And as soon as he reached New York, he forgot about his promise to repay the debt without fail.

'Right,' Zhenya said to himself. 'How can I believe in friendship after that? Maybe I should get a dog — at least it won't betray me.'

'Well, Zhenyek,' Sasha drawled as soon as he crossed the threshold, 'your flat looks as if it just about survived shelling. Where should we sit?' he asked as he walked from one room to another. 'In the living room? It looks more or less decent there.'

'I think in the living room. Let me just take off the plastic cover. I completely forgot about it, and to be honest, I didn't expect anyone to drop by.'

'Don't worry about that, it's alright.'

Zhenya started creating a nominal sense of order so he and his friend would have somewhere to sit. The room that bordered the kitchen was rather sparsely furnished, with a solitary sofa in the middle, a low glass-topped table, and a TV on the wall. Sasha put the bottle of whiskey on the table and sat down on the sofa. It was what he needed after the walk — to relax, drink some alcohol, and snack on a warm kebab. Alexander was glad that Zhenya, despite their almost year-long break in communication, had so easily and naturally agreed to spend the evening together.

'Well,' Evgeniy started, sitting next to Sasha on the sofa. 'Let's have a drink. Here's to our meeting; indeed, we haven't seen each other for a long time.'

'Let's,' Sasha responded, taking the bottle and pouring a drink for himself and his friend.

The whiskey was wonderful, its proof going unnoticed after the first glass.

'Another one?' Sasha suggested.

'Yep,' Zhenya agreed. 'What are we drinking to?'

'Let no one be able to betray us, because now we're prepared for that.'

'Nice toast! However, it sounds like the beginning of the story of why we're gathered here.'

Their glasses were empty again. Sasha reached out with

his right hand with a fork and dexterously picked a large piece of meat from a plastic container.

'Don't make me torture you, Alexander,' Zhenya said, looking at his friend reproachfully.

'I still can't gather my thoughts, you know,' Sasha replied. 'I don't even know where to start.'

'When did you break up with Ilona?'

'Right before the New Year; on the twenty-eighth of December, to be precise.'

'And how was it?'

'It was horrible; at least for me. You remember that we were going to get married, and I, just like in the case with the dog, procrastinated for too long, and she left me.'

'How? Just one day she decided to pick up and leave?' Zhenya asked.

'Of course not. We had a fight on the twentieth, then I realised that if I didn't propose I'd lose her forever. I bought a ring a long time ago, but it was difficult for me to take that step. In the end, on the twenty-eighth of December, I came to her house. I bought flowers and champagne. I took the ring, too. She came out. We talked. I tried to propose, and she turned me down.'

'I don't get it. She said "no"? Why?'

'Because the thing wasn't in the ring or the wedding. The reason was hidden so deeply, I only figured out Ilona's motives recently.'

'And what were they?'

'A month before the breakup, I began to catch myself thinking that we were arguing more and more often, moreover, about complete nonsense. That day, when we had the last fight, Ilona finally said what I'd been trying to figure out for myself but hadn't managed to. Literally, she said: "Sasha, I don't want to live like this. I need much, much more. I want to drive an expensive car, go to fancy restaurants, and only wear the best brand clothes. You, my darling, can't give any of that to me." There were many other things too, but these words, in particular, dug into my mind.'

'Wait, I don't get it; she said that as a complaint against you? And why did she decide you wouldn't be able to give all of that to her?'

'That's not even the point. She, as it turned out, only wanted money from me. But even after that, I somehow miraculously found the strength in myself and went to her to make an offer. But she still refused. You will laugh at why she did.

'Tell me,' Zhenya asked intently.

'Ilona wanted to start a new life, and she decided to go to St. Petersburg to earn more money. I have no idea what had got into her head, but she decided she'd make much more money there than I was paying her at my store.'

'What the hell?'

'Exactly, what the hell… What can I say? I was devastated. Please don't be offended, my friend, that I disappeared for a year. After the break-up with Ilona, I didn't want to see anybody. Tell me, how can I trust people now? I felt like with her actions, Ilona had not only made her own life null and void, but mine too.'

'Did she, though? On the contrary, it seems to me that

you should let her go. It doesn't mean you'll be alone for-ever - the more hook-ups, the higher the chance of finding another girl.'

'I don't want another girl,' Sasha said, smiling sadly. 'You see, after Ilona, I don't want to start a relationship. Maybe casual sex for a couple of nights, but that's it. I can't make myself, and I don't see the point.'

'It will pass, bro, believe me,' Zhenya said, patting his friend on the shoulder.

'Nope, Zhenya, I'm sorry, but I don't agree with you. If I was sixteen, of course, I'd suffer for a bit and then go back down that road again, but not now.'

'Have you changed your mind about starting a family?'

'To some extent, maybe I have. Just think about it — Ilona and I were in a relationship for three years. I loved her, and I thought she felt the same way about me. How many things have I done for her sake? The store never made any profit at all, and I only kept it open because that's what she wanted. But I'm not even talking about gifts, money, and all the rest. By the way, she even managed to rip me off before she left.'

'Rip you off? How?'

'It's simple. Ilona knew she was going to break up with me a month beforehand.'

'Why do you think that?'

'She took a ton of money from the till, and, as far as I can tell now, she used it to buy a plane ticket and to get started living in Peter[9]. That's how it is, bro. And if you think I'll sign up for that again, you've got to be joking.'

---

9   Peter – commonly used shortened name for Saint Petersburg.

'Sasha,' Evgeniy started calmly, 'firstly, you know very well that not all girls are like that. Secondly, I'm not saying you should run and marry the first you meet now; be smarter next time. And thirdly, even if you still have feelings for Ilona, and I can see that, you need to move on. There's no other way.'

'You're right, of course,' Alexander responded, scratching the back of his head and yawning. 'Though at this moment, the only one I can trust except my mum is Yoko. I know she'll never betray me and leave because she fell out of love with me. I'm immensely grateful to Ilona for the dog that became a real friend to me.'

'Does that mean you're completely disillusioned with people?'

'Not at all. I'll tell you this, though, henceforth, I'll only do what seems right to me. I won't adapt for anyone, especially girls. If she doesn't like something in me – farewell! If I notice she's only interested in money – cheerio! Spare me the nonsense and false promises given for one single purpose – to squeeze as much out of me as possible and then throw me in the trash can.

Sasha took the bottle and filled his glass to the brim. Exhaling, he knocked it back in one gulp and turning the glass bottom up on the table.

'Do you keep in touch with anyone at all?' Zhenya asked his friend timidly.

'You're the first one I've got in touch with. I thought of calling Kostya, but then forgot about it for some reason. I need to find out how he's doing. Though, on the other hand, taking into account his temper, he might not want to see me.'

'It's worth trying, at least,' Evgeniy said. 'Call him and see how it goes.'

'I'll call him tomorrow, then,' Sasha promised.

'It's interesting that you and Kostya live like within five hundred metres of each other and you often walk your dog there, yet you've never run into each other.'

'He's in the last year of his bachelor's degree, so he's likely sitting with his books even more than before. It's okay,' Alexander said determinately. 'I know he likes dogs very much, so I'll invite him for a walk with us. He won't refuse, for sure.'

***

Konstantin was lying on the sofa-bed in his room, but couldn't fall asleep. He was entirely overwhelmed with worries, which he started discussing with himself in a whisper.

'Why have I suddenly thought of her? So much time has passed already. No, there's no turning back, that's clear even to a fool. Still… what if there is such an opportunity and I just haven't thought of it? No, I tried every possible option, but I still didn't achieve my goal,' he rebuked himself. 'Even if I lost her, why did I start thinking of you, Tamara? It's strange, but sometimes it feels like you're thinking about me, too. I wish I could hold your hand and look into your cyes, which were always filled with love and sincerity, at least that's what I thought back then…'

He turned onto his right side, but it didn't help; his thoughts had no intention of leaving him alone.

'I remember every day we spent together; but why? What does it matter now? I wrote poems for you. Can you believe that? And you still banished me, telling me, "Konstantin, I don't love you." In which case, let me ask you this question? Did I ever treat you badly or act inappropriately? Didn't I try to spend every spare minute with you, giving you the most precious thing a man has — time?'

'What were those verses? Ah, damn, did I forget? Come on, make an effort to remember! I think it went:

'She didn't know what she could tell, and he would not accept rejection,
And time was floating into place, where both of them could be elated.
They could have feelings, though simply not for sheer exposition.
And possibly, too difficult to stop the flow of thoughts related.

A year has passed, all his attempts are clearly in vain,
There is no way to bring back what they had.
But he recalls that moment of the gentle embrace
That makes him skip a breath now and then.

And he could only guess which time would be desired,
And whether she would be available for him.

It might be that tonight,
She wouldn't come to meet him.

The sunset will be colouring the park in tints like a by-
gone dream,
The carillon will chime at seven and then fade away,
Let's try and start our love again from the beginning,
As if we fell in love once more and straight away.'

'Was it me who wrote that?' Konstantin asked himself.
'It's so weird to realise those verses were so amateurish.'

But even though they were lame, they kindled his mem-
ories.

He sat up on the sofa, his thoughts suddenly becoming
so clear, even too clear.

'No,' Kostya pronounced weightily. 'I guess I was in
love, but you can't really call it love. She simply decided to
play with me as if I were some kitten in the street, and didn't
take me home after that, leaving my heart in the cold.

'And it freezes and becomes colder day after day.

'Well, Toma[10], if that was your goal, then I have to admit, you succeeded. I tip my cap to you. Anyway, all I want
to say to you is "be happy," and I will try too.'

After Konstantin and Tamara broke up, the university
where they'd spent so many happy moments became associated with the fear of running into her.

Kostya understood that neither casual relationships, into
which he plunged from time to time, nor drunken evenings
in the company of classmates, nor sincere conversations

---

10   Toma is an abbreviated version of the name Tamara.

with relatives would help him completely forget his beloved. There was only one thing left — to hold out whatever it took, to overcome his raging emotions and graduate from the university. And then, who knows, maybe he'd never see Tamara again.

It was sometimes difficult for Kostya to accept the situation as it really was. It seemed as if people were striving to pique him and hurt him just when he least needed it. The thought that it might happen, that he, still such a young man, might live out his days in complete solitude was visiting him more and more often.

"If the people around me are hypocrites," Kostya would brood, "in no way does it mean I need to become like them. If they're able to turn away from me without a flicker of doubt, then it's their choice. But I don't think that I need to act like that.'

***

The next day, as evening was approaching, his phone rang. Konstantin noticed that the caller ID was unknown, and standing in the middle of the room, he was wondering hesitantly whether he should answer. Rejecting his doubts, he swiped his finger across the screen.

'Hello?'

'What's up, Kostya! How are you?'

Konstantin quickly realised it was Sasha on the other side of the line.

'Well, hello. Everything's alright, thank you. How are you?'

'All is well. What are you up to this evening?'

'I was planning to rest and watch a good movie.'

There was a short, silent pause.

'Listen,' Sasha started, 'do you fancy meeting up, say in a couple of hours?'

'Has something happened?' Kostya blurted automatically.

'Why do you ask?'

'We haven't talked for a year. It seemed to me that we ran out of topics of conversation.'

And then again, that awkward pause, only this time it was twice as long.

'So, I want to see you for a chat. What do you say?'

'Alright,' Kostya replied indifferently. 'Should I drive to you?'

'Yep-yep, do come! I'll see you at eight.'

'It's a deal.'

"That's strange," Kostya thought. "What got into Sasha's mind to meet up all of a sudden? I hope everything's alright with him. Though… a penny to a pound, he and Ilona have broken up. That's obvious. The only question is when."

He sighed deeply.

"We'll see what the meeting will bring."

Sitting in his car, for a moment Konstantin thought it was probably a bad idea to go there. What did he have to say to Sasha? They were never actually friends; they only communicated via Denis, and after his departure they tried to keep in touch, but failed.

"Let's assume," Kostya said to himself, "Sasha will say that Ilona and him have broken up. Okay, we'll discuss that. What next? We'll stop talking for another year, or maybe two? Why do I even need this?"

He got out of his car and immediately saw Sasha, who was walking slowly away from the entrance of his house. For a second, Kostya thought he saw a leash in his friend's hand, but he quickly banished this crazy thought.

"What kind of a vision is that?" he thought.

Sasha kept walking slowly, and the one that was trotting next to him, looking around at its owner at the same time, shocked Konstantin.

'What's up, Kostya?' Alexander asked, turning his eyes to Yoko. 'This is how we're doing now.'

'When did you get this fluffy miracle?'

'Almost a year ago. A couple of months after Den left.'

'What's her name?' Kostya asked.

'Yoko.'

'That's a name as beautiful as the bearer herself. I admit, I didn't see that coming at all,' Kostya laughed sincerely. 'I thought that you and Ilona had separated and that's why you decided to call me after a year.'

'We did separate,' Sasha said without any emotion on his face. 'Why did you think that?'

'You think I didn't notice that we were only communicating via Den? After his departure, you disappeared, and I thought it was only logical. But the fact you've reappeared is interesting.'

'Why logical? Could you clarify, please?' Alexander asked, dumbfounded.

'Well, Ilona was dead set against Denis, who, according to her, was dragging you off to cheat on her with other girls. After he left, I realised that Sanya would drop off the radar. Ilona and you were in a committed relationship; you were going to get married. And what have I got to do with that? We were never great friends, at least not as close as you were with Denis. Therefore, everything that transpired seemed quite logical to me, as I said.'

'Yeah, we were in a serious relationship,' Sasha said after a five-second pause.

'Right,' Kostya said, sounding distant. 'Will you tell me what happened, or aren't you ready yet?'

'Shall we go for a walk or what? Yoko needs to do her business anyway. I'll tell you on the way.'

The weather was excellent. The light evening coolness gradually filling the city air created a wonderful mood which made any activity more cheerful. Reaching the crossroad, the three of them stopped at the traffic lights. Kostya didn't take his eyes off of his fluffy friend, who seemed equally enamoured with him.

Konstantin noted that Yoko, who'd won his heart over the second they were introduced, was acting like an English lady with her inherent manners. He was used to seeing dogs barking when meeting a new person, even though the barking was often quite happy and excited. Not in this case, though; Yoko only came up to him at a leisurely pace, sniffed him and lifted her snout as if to say: 'He's okay,' and sat on the asphalt looking in the other direction. With all this formal behaviour, Kostya suddenly hooked out one of the thousand thoughts that were hectically rushing through his mind – even if Sasha and he weren't real friends, if he wanted to be in touch again, he wouldn't mind. Only a few years later did Konstantin realise that he wasn't opposed to spending time with Yoko, and it didn't matter who her owner was.

Reaching the park, where one could see couples wandering around and single people, most often walking their dogs at any time of the day, Sasha released the leash to the full and gave Yoko the opportunity to run around a bit. Kostya wasn't even thinking of breaking the silence because he knew first-hand how difficult it was to start a story about the one who used to be the most precious person in the world to you.

'Look how Yoko loves the lawn; she tends to run on the grass. Asphalt is no good for her anymore; right?' Sasha said, turning to his most loyal friend. 'What would I do without you, Yoko?' he uttered with a touch of melancholy.

Taking a cigarette from the pack, he lit it hurriedly.

'I've also been thinking about getting a dog for a long time, but I still can't do it.'

'What's so difficult?' Sasha asked ironically.

'It's a huge responsibility. A puppy demands a lot of attention, and because I'm busy with my studies, I wouldn't be able to take care of it properly. Besides, I have an elderly grandma at home; and puppies are silly, you can't explain to them that there's an elderly person at home for whom those snappy somersaults under their feet wouldn't be appropriate, and they're not like me, who is young and full of energy. But as soon as I get a house of my own, I'll get a dog — that much I've decided.'

'Finally, someone besides me understands that! I kept telling Ilona the same thing when she pleaded incessantly with me to bring a puppy home.'

'Wow,' Kostya said. 'So, it was her who made you get Yoko?'

'You know, I'm not even sure now that it was like that.'

'What do you mean?'

'Sure, Ilona nagged me for a long time, but I can't say that she made me get Yoko. Looking back, I understand that in that period of my life, I needed a real friend like never before. I probably realised that in the depths of my heart, but the acknowledgement of the fact only came recently.'

'Will you tell me why you disappeared for a whole year?' Kostya asked directly.

'How should I tell you so you won't get offended? And for that matter… well, I didn't want to see anybody, you see? Neither friends nor acquaintances — absolutely nobody. I had days when I just lay on the sofa and drank beer. Even Yoko was walked by my mother, I was so sad.'

'And how did you get rid of the melancholy?'

'In the evening on one such day, I got up from the sofa and heard my dog quietly yelping in the adjacent room. I went there and saw how her face immediately transformed — Yoko looked at me with her loyal eyes, in which I saw everything I needed back then.'

'Yeah,' Kostya said thoughtfully, 'dogs feel everything and love us the way we are, without pretty clothes, beautiful perfume, and money in our pockets. Probably when I am completely done with people, and even if I don't buy a house by then, I'll let it all hang out and get a dog. And something tells me that it might happen quite soon.'

'You're right. I got a dog because I stopped seeing sincerity and kindness in people. I have a decent attitude towards myself, which is logical because I'm not an evil person. Here's the important thing, though: no one person can fully understand another. There will never come a moment in a relationship when you can say with confidence: I know who she is, what she'll do, and what she'll strive towards,' Sasha said, drawing deeply on his cigarette. 'One time was enough for me.'

'To tell you the truth, I have the same opinion about people, but I can't say that I would never be able to trust anyone. Well, at least with some banal things, yes, sure, but personal feelings and worries, of course, not.'

'And rightly so. All your faults the other person, as it turns out, has to endure and doesn't accept as something implicit will be used against you the moment you've fully trusted them, and when you least expect that.'

'And would you want to get her back?' Kostya asked sharply.

'That's a good question. Even if I did want that, Ilona wouldn't necessarily want to try again. She told me she "wanted more."'

'That's strange. So, what has actually happened?'

'She went to St. Petersburg and decided to start a new life there. She wanted to prove something to herself and maybe to me too, but I still can't figure out what exactly. I created all the conditions she wanted here in Tashkent. She wanted to be a clothing store manager, so I kept the company afloat; she wanted to have vacations, so we travelled. There was no problem with that either. She waited for a proposal – I did that, but she refused, saying it was over.'

'You proposed to her?' Kostya repeated with a wide-mouth and with round eyes.

'Yeah, I did,' Sasha uttered glumly, and jerked Yoko's leash. 'Hey dog, what are you dragging me for? We were walking alright.'

Yoko didn't even respond. She looked at her owner with her brown eyes and kept on sniffing, like a pathfinder, sniffing everything that was on her way.

'Well,' Konstantin spoke wistfully, 'that's why I'm not going to marry anyone,' and he burst into hysterical laughter.

'And you're right, Kostya – you're too young. And in general, how did our parents manage to find each other, get married and have children?'

'I often ask myself this question,' Kostya replied. 'They lived in a different time; they had different values. It's not like now. Just look, when you get on social media, what do you see there? Their half-naked bodies' girls post or some sham-smart thoughts which aren't even their own! Moreover, they have the audacity to outline their demands to guys. I'd like to ask them one question — what can you, chicken, offer a young man besides your body? And they know they have nothing. But do they do anything to raise their level of intelligence from that dumb pit of ignorance? No! It's gonna end badly.'

'Why? There are a lot of rich and not-so-smart young men who are only interested in one-night stands. If there's a demand, there's a supply. Market economics, dear friend. That's our world; what can we do?'

'Change it. Though I agree with you; I doubt I can change anything. But I won't let anyone take away my right to create my own world. Let it be unrealistic, but in any case, I prefer it to prostitutes who call themselves models. In this world, there are still such concepts as friendship, love, and sincerity. And those ladies of the night, let them stand at the stalls of the market of carnal delights.'

That evening, which began with Konstantin's scepticism, was the first of its kind, but it led to regular events which in this context could be called 'walking the dog'.

Time, as you know, only flows in one direction. Too often, Kostya, and perhaps Sasha too, wanted to return to the life they'd had a few years earlier. But mistakes or situations which had occurred ended up having too strong an impact to be forgotten overnight.

It's funny how sometimes the hours spent with this or that person convince us that this person will become a friend with whom we'll keep in touch until the end of our days. Yes, Kostya had probably never been so wrong.

The phone started ringing. Konstantin was taking a shower and decided that whoever it was, they weren't going to get out from under the warm, flowing water.

"I'll call them later," he decided.

Putting on his bathrobe, Kostya left the bathroom and went to his room. Sitting on his grey sofa, he started thinking about Tamara, who wouldn't leave his mind.

"That's strange," he thought. "I clearly understand there's no way back, that this story is over, but I still keep thinking about her day after day, as if it's just the distance between our houses that separates us, and not the abyss of misunderstanding."

'Maybe I should bury my pride somewhere deep inside and go to her?' he said aloud. 'Despite the things she said when we saw each other last, I really want to see her!

'On the other hand, I'm aware that this attempt, like many others, would turn out to be counterproductive,' he ruminated. 'At least now I clearly understand the essence of the situation I find myself in. Tamara doesn't know what she wants, neither at present nor in the future. Well, it's probably her lack of experience, which I took as an advantage, but no, it's not. A person must have experience; especially the negative ones, because only this can open one's eyes to the good attitude that is so often taken for granted.

'Right, I must stop thinking about you, Toma. Enough of this depressing attitude. It's time to move forward, and who knows, maybe I'll get lucky again and find a person with whom I want to spend my life.'

Finishing his monologue, Kostya recalled the missed phone call. Unwillingly, he got up from the sofa and approached the light-brown desk. The missed call was from Sasha.

"That means we're going for a walk today," Konstantin thought, and dialled the number.

'Hello, Sash. Did you call me?'

'Hi-hi; how are you?'

'Not bad, thanks. What's up with you?'

'Yeah, everything's fine. Listen, what are you up to tonight?'

'Not much, really. What are you suggesting?'

'Do you remember Aziz?'

'Of course I do. Anything happened to him?'

'No, everything's fine; don't worry. He's become the manager of one of the country clubs. They have everything there — saunas, swimming pools, cottages, decent food. But it's spring now, and the season hasn't started yet, so officially they're not open yet and only preparing to open at the end of May or the beginning of June. He invited me, and I'm calling you. So, are you coming?'

'How long would we be there?'

'We'll get back to Tashkent around two or three in the morning. It'll take us thirty or forty minutes to get there. You know what, let's go for a walk with Yoko, and then one of us will get behind the wheel and we'll go to Aziz. We'll have dinner there, too.'

'This is an excellent plan! I haven't been out in nature for ages. What time are we meeting?'

'Drive or walk to me by half-past seven. Only grab some warm clothes — it's cool in the evening out of town.'

Kostya arrived at the agreed time. Sasha and Yoko were hurriedly walking out of the house as if they were late for something.

'Good evening, Sanya.'

'Evening. Let's go for a quick walk with her and then head for the Riviera. The pilau is cooking already.'

That day, the walk, which usually lasted for at least two hours, took not more than half an hour. Yoko didn't complain — the temperature in Tashkent was inevitably growing day by day with the approach of summer, which was always boiling. The breed that Yoko belonged to was used to a moderate, even rather cold climate, which was the polar opposite to Uzbekistan.

'Will you drive or me?' Sasha asked.

'I don't know; it doesn't matter really,' Kostya drawled.

'Let's decide this quick. The pilau will get cold, and the billiards won't play itself without us.'

'Are you going to drink?'

'Well, I wouldn't mind a couple of beers if you don't mind driving us back home,' Sasha said, smiling cunningly.

'Alright then, we'll go in my car. I don't know the route, though.'

'You know it. It's on the way to the Barrel. I'll tell you when to turn.'

'Then finish smoking and let's go,' Kostya commanded.

There were a lot of cars on the road. Konstantin, who did not go out of town often, was slightly surprised by the fact they got stuck in a traffic jam a few kilometres before the Rokhat[11] station.

'It's Friday,' Sasha said calmly. 'Everyone's headed out of town — some returning to their regions, and some, like us, going to the mountains to have a break.'

'You know, when I didn't have a car, I thought: "I wish I could start driving and go to the mountains, to Charvak every week… It's so beautiful there!" And in the end, I have a car, but there are a lot more things to do all day, which doesn't make you go anywhere in the evening.'

'You sound like a pensioner! Stop that now,' Sasha replied, laughing.

'Well, everything points to that,' Kostya uttered, smiling and staring at the road. 'I have old-fashioned opinions; you can't argue with that.'

'The fact is that adequate people are out of fashion now, and we've already discussed that. That doesn't mean you need to adapt to the modern age, though.'

'Of course. But look, say you're going on a date with a girl. She is pretty and hot, her figure is right, her face is pretty, well-groomed — that's what you see. Suppose you're sitting at a table, talking, and you suddenly realise she's talking complete nonsense. In my head, the option for the continuation of communication immediately disappears, and a new one appears, which is designed, by and large, for one night. And then you leave her or take her home, and that's it — you're done. Maybe, if she's really stupid, you have to respond several times to her attempts to open a line

---

11   Rokhat – a traffic control point for cars at the entrance to Tashkent.

of communication again because she doesn't understand the simplest thing — you're no longer interested. I'd like to find, first of all, a good interlocutor in a girl with whom sex will fade into the background, because she'll be something more than a beautiful shell. So, you're right; I fully justify the title of retiree.

'Come on, I'm just kidding, forget it,' Sasha said soulfully. 'You are, of course, right about all of this. Only where can I find such a girl? All those girls who I can talk about anything with are either hideous, like my ex's life, or have bats in their belfry I have to run for my life from! By the way, something happened recently; oh, you'll be knocked for six.'

'Tell me. You've already built-up the suspense,' Kostya said, as they slowly passed by a city bridge.

'Well, I started texting a lady on a dating site, naturally, without any serious intentions, just to kill some time. She was quite adequate in her communication, so we exchanged numbers and talked several times. These were long talks until late at night, on occasion. So, I suggested meeting in reality.

'We agreed on a date, and I came to the place, found the parking lot and sat in the car smoking. Half an hour passed, an hour, and she still hadn't shown up. I was about to leave when I saw her number on the screen of my phone; she was standing opposite the park where we'd agreed to meet.

'So, I left the parking lot as the park was closing. At the traffic lights, I made a U-turn and passed by the place where she was standing. I evaluated her, and something clicked in me; for a second, I thought, "What the hell! Maybe I should leave?"

'But I stayed, and drove up to her, and got out of the car. Her name was Lera, I think. So… we looked at each other and then she said: "I'm sorry for being late. Someone has been following me - that's why I was afraid to leave the house." I asked who, but she didn't answer.

'Okay, I thought, all the fun was about to start. I suggested we go for a walk around the catholic church, and she starts talking about some coincidences and that she can foresee things, but whenever I asked for any clarification, I got the sense she obviously had a few marbles missing. I needed to wrap it up.

'It was quite late, so I offered her a ride home without any hidden agenda. Lera looked at me as if I were a lunatic and said: "I don't get into strangers' cars." Can you imagine? We'd just been walking at night around a district that was deserted and fairly unknown to her! Okay, I thought, and said, "Whatever you say." I got into my car and drove to the traffic lights, turned round, parked on the opposite side of the street and waited.

'Lera was trying to get a taxi, but there weren't many cars around. This went on for about fifteen minutes before I decided to make another round and try to offer her a ride home. Again, I was doing this in all innocence — I just wanted to act like a gentleman who'd never leave a dame in such a situation.

'She rejected my offer for another twenty minutes or so before agreeing to get in. I gave her a lift, but then she said she wanted to get out and walk the rest of the way as she didn't want me to know where she lived. I said: "Alright." Lera walked away into the night, and I got out for a smoke, threw away the cigarette butt, and drove home as fast as possible. And my question for you is: What do you think happened next?'

'Hmm,' Kostya murmured thoughtfully, 'I'm afraid to assume that nothing happened, right?'

'I wish. That freak started texting and calling me, even when I was at work or busy with my business. Somehow she'd decided we were strongly attracted to each other and now we were going to date. I didn't want to offend her and tried to explain everything nicely — we have different paths to follow, babe.

'Well, that didn't work. Alright, I thought, I'll do it another way. I started ignoring her calls and messages. That didn't work either. So as much as I hate putting people on the blacklist, I had to do it with her. And what do you think happened? She changed her number and continued terrorising me!'

'Oh, come on,' Kostya said, smirking. 'The girl liked you; you hooked her, as they say. What's wrong with that?'

'It's that she absolutely fails to realise what she's doing and saying. Why would she do all that bullshit?'

'Who knows?' Konstantin waved away the question. 'How did the classic writer say it: "The less we love a woman…" So, don't panic. You got a bit of a strange girl, but so what?'

'It looks like only the likes of her are on these dating

sites. I need to delete my profile; there's nothing for me there!'

'Are you serious? Interesting. I visit such websites and run into inadequate ladies, too. But it's fun! At least we have stories we can laugh at. It's better than nothing.'

'Is it?' Sasha replied sadly.

'I can tell by the look on your face that you're still thinking about Ilona.'

'Yes, but what else can I do?'

'First, try to get her back.'

'Oh, you're so clever! What would I do without you?'

'Yep,' Konstantin laughed.

'But seriously,' Sasha started, 'I do think about it quite often. There are different options in my head, and one is better than the others. I know how to organise it. There are no material or any other obstacles for me. The only thing that keeps gnawing at me is why should I ask her to come back after she wiped the floor with me? Does that mean that I need her more than she needs me? I can't; and it's not just a matter of pride. After all we had between us, after everything I did for Ilona's sake she just left me, choosing an unknown that was absolutely incomprehensible to me. I still know everything about her — where she works, what she does, who she's in touch with,' Sasha said, ticking the items off with his fingers. 'You should understand that I don't need to be a genius to get Ilona back. Everything is plain and predictable. But you tell me now, why you don't get back with Tamara? What's holding you back? You also loved her so much, had strong feelings, call it whatever you want! Answer this question, then you'll understand me.'

Kostya turned his head and looked at his friend attentively. He could see that Sasha wanted to smoke.

'Light a cigarette if you want,' Konstantin said. 'We're driving with the windows open, anyway. The smoke will blow away.'

'Thanks,' Sasha muttered almost inaudibly.

'Yes, you're right, I loved Toma. Maybe I still have feelings for her, but I don't want to start our relationship over again. I did everything I could. The problem was, she didn't know what she wanted. Not just from me, but from life in general.

'Would it be worth stepping on the same rake without any confidence that the result would change? I don't think so. As much as I'd like to, I can't get inside her head and understand the logic behind her actions. Maybe one day we'll meet, but at the moment there's no point.'

'You know what I'm happy for right now despite all the things that are happening in my life?' Sasha asked.

'Of course not,' Kostya replied seriously. 'Enlighten me.'

'I'm immensely happy I have Yoko, and for that I'll be always grateful to Ilona. When you get a dog, when you consciously make this decision and get it, you'll probably understand what I mean. A dog is the only creature that will love you no matter how you look, what mood you're in, how things are going for you, or whether you are rich or poor. It doesn't matter to Yoko…

'When Ilona left - I've probably already told you this - on one of the days I was drinking, I suddenly saw a whole world in the eyes of my Yoko, who is much more than a dog to me. Yoko means so much to me because I take care of her, and, even if I don't like this word, I'm her "owner." For her, I'm an immense and boundless universe that she can't help but to love.

'In my relationship with Ilona, I was investing so much strength, time, and money. And what was the result? She just turned around and left. If there was a single meaningful reason, I could understand that; I'm not dumb. But there wasn't.

'So, what would be the point in giving my attention to her again if she could simply wipe the floor with me again despite having achieved nothing herself? No; or at least I'm not ready to do that now. With time, I won't deny it, people's attitudes change, and we change too. But what I can say with a hundred percent confidence is the chances that someone else would tolerate Ilona's temper are poor. And it's true, if there is such a man, I would wish them both all the happiness in the world. However, from what I can see in her life, the outlook is very sad.'

'You know what the most ridiculous thing in our situations is? We see things the way they are, analyse them and make thorough observations… yet we keep discussing Ilona and Tamara!' Kostya said, laughing out loud.

'Right,' said Sasha. 'Slow down a bit here. Our U-turn will be coming up soon.'

Having turned in the designated area, Kostya drove in the opposite direction.

It was so good to be out of the city. The crystal-clear air blowing through the windows seemed to free their minds from the captivity of their obsessions, which, no doubt, were Ilona and Tamara.

Having driven into the courtyard where the rows of private dachas began, Kostya followed the instructions of his friend, who'd been here before. Reaching the big red metal gates, Konstantin wanted to park the car in a vacant spot, but Sasha said they would open the gates for them, and they would park inside.

'Hey, Seryi, where's Azizka?' Sasha asked merrily. 'We've come to eat your pilau. Are you accepting guests?'

'Hello, Sasha. How are you?'

'Everything's fine. Where is our fatty?'

'He's on the phone. You can go in and take a walk if you want. We'll sit at the table in about twenty minutes.'

'Excellent! I'll show my friend around then. Ah, I completely forgot — Seryi, let me introduce my friend Kostya.'

Kostya and Seryi shook hands.

'Well, we'll go then,' Sasha said. 'Call me when the king is in the castle,' he added, laughing.

The grounds of the Riviera were impressive. There were six or seven acres of well-groomed land, the majority of which was taken up by cottages, swimming pools, and other buildings. Lights were on in the windows of the houses they passed. There was greenery everywhere, which would be a saviour on the hottest summer days, which would soon to come.

Walking the grounds, Kostya was amazed — right in the middle of the lawn there were two dwarf ponies grazing, a boy and a girl. He stopped dead and stayed like that until he shifted his gaze further and exclaimed,

'Are those camels?'

There was a tiny zoo on the territory of the Riviera. It was, of course, illegal, but who cared? Definitely not Konstantin, who was quite bewildered.

'Look around… isn't it great?' Alexander asked. 'It's so peaceful here… I love coming here.'

'I feel a real sense of peace at this place.'

'That's why I love coming to Riviera so much - all of your troubles recede here! You admire nature, communicate with these wonderful animals, and when you go back, your problems in the present no longer seem insoluble.'

'It's certainly a good place to think,' Kostya agreed. 'I need to find time to come here more often.'

'You can always find time; you know that. The main thing is you must want to.'

Evening smoothly segued into night, adding to the allure of the place. Having walked around the perimeter, they turned back towards their car in silence when Sasha's phone started buzzing in his pocket — it was Aziz saying they were gathering at the table.

Dinner in a big company… it had been so long Kostya had forgotten how such things happen. There were discussions at the table that could turn into heated but friendly arguments, and everything around was filled with unsurpassable charm tinged with a hint of melancholy which was caused by the inevitability of parting.

Standing by the billiards table watching Aziz and Sasha play a game, Kostya felt a state of happiness achieved through small things formed exactly the way they should be. Putting the billiard cue back in its place, he shook Aziz's hand and thanked him for such a wonderful reception, and in return heard these warm words: 'Come again, guys. We'd be happy to see you.'

The road home always seems shorter for some reason. We already know everything and just want to get back.

'Thank you, Sash,' Kostya said gratefully.

'What for?' his friend responded in surprise.

'For taking me to the Riviera. I have strange thoughts in my head right now, but I'd like to formulate and express them.'

'Go ahead,' Sasha said, smiling wearily and lying back on the car seat.

Konstantin began to piece the evening together. There was not a single detail that could spoil the indescribable impression.

'You know, Sash, let it sound a bit sentimental, but I truly want to remember us like that: young and ready to cut loose and come to the Riviera. Yes, we have problems. Yes, we periodically think about our ex-girlfriends who won't let go of our hearts. However, I want to remember you like this — you go out with Yoko, we walk and talk heart-to-heart, and she trots next to us silently supporting our conversation.

I want to remember myself standing next to my car knowing that in a few moments you two are going to appear from your house, and we'll set off on our daily journey which, despite the familiar route, shimmers in my memory with completely different colours every time.'

Chapter Three
Life after

"And again, a person disappears from my life," Kostya thought, sitting at the wheel of his car late one evening.

Sometimes it seemed the next day would bring nothing new and only leave him alone with the fears which had seized power in the kingdom of his thoughts. At first, Konstantin believed that other people were to blame for everything. He wanted to think they'd led to his current state, in which he felt nobody needed him. Days like these, which had turned into weeks and months, were a test of his character. Awareness often only comes later, and at times not at all.

Konstantin started having the same rather weird dream. In these visions, he was either stood in the middle of the street, was sitting on the sofa in his room, or was walking somewhere aimlessly. But wherever he was, the major feature was the crowd, which followed him everywhere.

It usually started like this: Kostya was completely alone, which became unbearable, because no matter where he looked, no matter how hard he tried to find at least one person, all his attempts were in vain. Then he closed his eyes and began to quietly read the prayer he usually said before going to bed. At the end of it, he opened his eyes and was shocked — a dense crowd had appeared around him, representing a unified whole. He tried to discern individual faces, but they, having turned into the outlines of friends, acquaintances and beloved girls, disappeared and became part of a human stream, which dissipated at the moment the alarm clock rang at the designated hour in the morning.

At first, Kostya woke up in a cold sweat and with rather unusual feelings, but he didn't want to think about these extraordinary dreams and, even more so, about their sacral meaning. He had graduated from the university and it was necessary to decide what to do next, but according to some internal order, Konstantin was in no hurry to look for a job, which many of his classmates were already doing. The thought that this would be resolved one way or another was firmly planted in his head. And indeed, in the end, it turned out well, for using his connections, Kostya found employment in a good company, and, moreover, in his specialty, and went to work the very next day after defending his thesis. The thought that everything in life would turn out the way it should be made Konstantin wonder about the message that was hidden in his dreams.

One Saturday night, Kostya suddenly decided to drink some alcohol.

"I can pour myself some whiskey," he thought, "but I don't want to get drunk, so I'll just have a sip."

'So,' he said aloud, 'Perhaps I'll open a bottle of wine instead and switch on some life-asserting film.'

Kostya poured some red wine into a glass and started searching for a movie on his laptop, the title of which he couldn't recall.

"The main thing isn't the name," he thought. "It's the atmosphere that overwhelms you as soon as you press the 'play' button."

Sunday morning turned out to be unbearably lonely. Konstantin felt there were some unperceivable changes going on in him, as if the old mechanisms made from impermanent materials were being replaced with more durable ones. He had only to wait until the renovations were finished to try studying the new, still unknown possibilities of his mindset.

The gears started moving quickly, even too quickly, as Konstantin recalled later. A lot of things he had been brooding about during the long sleepless nights were suddenly replaced by obvious facts which easily settled into his updated understanding of everyday life.

Placing a clean sheet of paper in front of himself, he started writing.

"Everything this or that person does in life – they do only for themself.

Love and self-sacrifice are two inextricably linked concepts, but the nature of their association becomes illusory when certain life circumstances develop in such a way that the concept of 'partner' acquires an indisputably authoritative meaning.

Friendship and self-sacrifice are two independent variables, which, although sometimes in the same matrix equation of being, the presence or absence of one of them does not entail cardinal changes in the final protocol of the resulting vector.

Family and self-sacrifice are a complicated system comprised of many equations, of which there are always more than unknowns. Therefore, this system has a solution for any value within the initial parameters.

Self-sacrifice is an axiomatic concept inherent in human nature, which does not carry any meaning without specific reference to certain circumstances.

Disappointment is the most likely outcome of any expectation associated with certain reactions from another person. The less we expect, the sweeter the gestures of benevolence received from strangers.

External beauty is an independent measure, the meaning of which is quite abstract. The most important thing is that it is in no way obliged to have an intersection with mental abilities, and most often serves as a vulgar tool for achieving goals.

Inner beauty, in its turn, defines the ability of a man to be in charge of his time, and the more effective this process is, the faster that beautiful rose grows inside a virgin garden hidden behind the outer shell."

"Yeah," Konstantin thought, "I have enough brains to understand all this, but why does it seem to me that I'm incredibly alone in my reasoning?"

He was working diligently - more because of an irrepressible interest in the process rather than the call of the rustling banknotes. He had a lot to do, and with time his workload only increased as the trust the management put in him grew at an exponential rate.

One evening, exhausted, Kostya was slowly but steadily approaching his house. Passing through a park where he'd spent so much time together with Sasha and Yoko, he absently glanced at the empty grove and immediately cheered up, for there among the trees he spotted two familiar figures. It was Alexander and his loyal friend Yoko.

"Well, thank God," Kostya thought. "Everything is fine with them, even without me."

Wonderful is that moment of awareness when one realises: so, the world doesn't revolve around me. Does that mean if I leave, nothing will change? Perhaps it does. So, loneliness is my path.

When we communicate with a person, we begin to become attached and our expectations, even the most insignificant ones, grow over time like a weed in the thinking organ until we have to uproot them. This procedure is very painful, but without it we run the risk of becoming dependent on another, which, in turn, leads to no less depressing consequences.

Having realised many things, Konstantin stopped giving advice to others, became laconic, would answer only if directly asked, and was cordially silent when listening to the absurdities espoused by those around him. He repeatedly admitted to himself that this strategy was the most effective because people, no matter how much they want to hide it, look forward to the reaction to their reasoning in order to either accept praise and recognise the interlocutor as equal to themselves, or bring down an inexhaustible arsenal of scorn on those who disagree. Silence in such a situation is a shield, which, after some time, turns into a terrible weapon in the enraged imagination of the opponent, from which there is no escape.

Night. The sacred darkness and time for one of the most intimate processes — the unification of a man with his bed and pillow. Sometimes a blanket joins this trio, and in the cold of winter is greeted with outstretched arms, before being tossed aside as the inevitable heat approaches.

Phone. Why does he call when all thoughts about him have completely faded away? The result is one missed call. Kostya switched off the phone and wearily fell back into bed. He was not in the mood to chat with Alexander.

"That's okay," Kostya thought; "I'll call him back tomorrow."

He didn't, though, and he didn't attach much significance to it, either.

"He'll call again," Konstantin told himself. "He hasn't shown up for six months, so one call won't change anything."

And again he plunged himself into his work, setting new goals and toiling from Monday to Sunday.

Exhausted after a productive working week, Konstantin lazily lay on the sofa watching some movie.

His phone rang. Kostya calmly looked at it and sighed deeply: it was Sasha.

"Alright, I'm not like him,' Kostya thought; 'I don't have that habit of disappearing."

'Hi!'

'Hi,' Kostya replied nonchalantly.

'So, how are you?' Sasha asked, sounding like there were some new notes in his voice which were unusual for him.

'Ah well, alright. What about you?' Konstantin continued in the same nonchalant manner.

'The usual life. Do you mind meeting up? Say today?'

'Hmm, alright, let's try again,' Kostya agreed reluctantly.

'At eight?'

'Okay.'

Hanging up the phone, Konstantin vented his emotions.

'Why is he calling me? What does he want to say to me? Why should I silently accept as normal such behaviour from him? No… I'll tell him everything I think about our so-called 'friendship' and everything connected with it. That's enough! I'm ready to be alone. It's better than being with any Tom, Dick, or Harry.

The chiming clock that was a kilometre away from Alexander's house started beating the time. On the eighth beat, the door opened, and Sasha appeared in front of Konstantin with a leash in his hand.

'Come on, what's with you?' he said to something hidden by the darkness of the entrance. 'Let's go, you cowardly little girl.'

There was no movement. Then Sasha, holding the door with his left foot, bent down and took something into his arms. Kostya silently watched the scene unfold, whilst preparing to pour out his anger and resentment towards the man he'd so naively considered to be his friend. He restrained himself, though; and the point wasn't that Kostya had suddenly mastered his emotions, but what he saw. It was a puppy - tiny, and far from fully formed. It raised its little eyes to the new person, and its face took on the expression of sincere, childish interest.

'Well, Aiko, go and meet uncle Kostya,' Alexander uttered sadly.

Collecting all his strength so he wouldn't cry at the moment, Konstantin stopped, frozen to the spot. The tiny white and ginger ball ran up to him and clumsily started examining this new acquaintance. As if enchanted, Kostya took the puppy in his arms and started stroking it. Suddenly, Aiko looked into his eyes as if feeling the pain that pierced the young man through and through. In that look, Konstantin read: "I know everything. She can't be returned. Now I'm your new friend."

Calmly putting the dog on the ground, Kostya wanted to take a step towards Sasha, but Aiko didn't consider it appropriate and kept jumping and wriggling, attracting as much attention as possible.

'She's just like a child,' Konstantin said to himself.

He tried to take her into his arms when he heard and then saw a little trickle of joy that Aiko had decided to greet him with.

'Aiko,' Sasha said faux-strictly. 'And what is that?'

Pulling the leash and scalding the puppy, which couldn't understand what it had done wrong, Sasha addressed Kostya:

'I'm sorry, she's still a baby. She pees with joy sometimes, as you can see.'

Kostya was silent. Could he say anything at all? What he had been thinking a few minutes ago became so unimportant and far from reality that he, being frustrated, tried to find the right lever in his brain so it would start running smoothly.

'Maybe we should go for a walk?' Alexander suggested. 'Otherwise, she'll mark everything here.'

They walked along the same paths, the same trees, fences, and curbs. The details that Kostya didn't consider important before, that he didn't take into account, now became the centre of his attention.

"Why is he so calm?" was the question pounding in Konstantin's head. "Isn't there anything human left in him? I'd like to believe in the unbelievable… to believe Yoko just stayed at home, but there's no use in that hope.

"She died, my friend! So silent and even arrogant, not letting me stroke her at our first meeting — yes, it was true, but I loved her so much and my heart was really pounding with joy at the moment when I saw them in the park. Why didn't I call out to him that day? Again, damned pride! Though, no," he rebuked himself. "That was common sense. How would it have helped me?"

The silence that Alexander and Konstantin observed while walking around Tashkent that evening was a balm for both souls. Breaking it would mean they risked shedding bitter tears for the one they both loved, each in his own way. Although he'd seen enough deaths in his life, Kostya doubted he'd be able to live through that.

"It's impossible to stay the same as you were before you met your first dog," he thought.

An hour and a half passed. Sasha was walking calmly next to him, smoking one cigarette after another, and Kostya was plunging ever deeper into his own thoughts, now and then throwing glances at Aiko and catching her eyes. They approached the house - returning to the starting point since when it seemed to Kostya that an eternity had passed.

'Listen, Kostya… do you mind if we walk to my dad's cottage nearby? I want to drink and chat so much.'

Konstantin silently nodded in response. He needed to reboot his system.

After a couple of minutes, Sasha came downstairs with a bottle of dark brown drink in his hands. Konstantin didn't care what they drank, because the choice of alcohol, like other signs of material reality, mattered nothing to him. The massive metal door to the courtyard squeaked mildly before giving in to its owner's touch and opening.

Stepping into the courtyard, Konstantin, who might have admired the building or the perfect lawn, stood in a daze, realising that somewhere here - perhaps under his feet - lay Yoko's body. Noticing the state of his friend, Sasha went to the annex where his father's office was situated. Having found the right key in the bunch, he opened the door and disappeared into the darkness, returned a minute later with glasses and folding chairs. Putting everything on the concrete steps, he went down to the basement and brought up a small plastic table. Without saying a word, Kostya took the table in his hands and looked inquiringly at Sasha – who silently pointed to a spot near the empty pool.

Sitting down, Sasha clumsily opened a bottle and pulled the glasses closer. Pouring the whiskey into them, he silently handed one to his friend.

Kostya raised his glass and solemnly said: 'To Yoko.'

They drank, and then again, and again.

'How did it happen?' Konstantin asked in a barely audible voice.

Alexander drew on a cigarette and exhaled loudly.

'I'll start from the beginning, Kostya; from the moment we stopped communicating.

'You disappeared, and for some reason I didn't attach much importance to that, though I was probably wrong. I decided you needed time, and I obviously did, too.'

Kostya kept silent, though. It was not the best moment for finger-pointing.

'We walked in the evenings, as usual,' Sasha continued. 'Everything was stable and normal. As always, in short. I started hanging out with Zhenya occasionally. He came by now and then, and the three of us went for a walk.

'One afternoon, I went out with Yoko. I came home for lunch overloaded with problems and wanted to make amends for not taking her out that morning that day. Having reached the kindergarten - well, you know where it is - Yoko suddenly fell.'

It was clear from the look on his face what he'd gone through that day.

'She just fell,' he repeated mechanically, 'and started breathing heavily. I grabbed her in my arms, ran to my car as fast as I could, and drove Yoko to the vets. I remember driving like crazy: I ran a red light and almost got into an accident, but miraculously I made it to the clinic alive. I burst into it with mad eyes filled with powerlessness and incomprehension. The vet recognised me and rushed to us; he obviously knew it was serious.

'Then everything is a blur. I smoked outside, pacing back and forth. I felt a sharp pain in my chest that almost double over. I had a feeling in my guts and ran inside. The doctor walked towards me, and it was enough to look at his face — they couldn't save her. I was too late. The drive was too long.

'Though no; that's not true. Yoko had internal bleeding, and it was impossible to help her. After that, I don't remember anything until the moment when my father and I dug her grave,' he said, turning and pointing at a hillock where flowers were growing already. 'We buried Yoko there,' he added quietly. 'She's not with us anymore. That's the story, bro… that's the story.'

Kostya slowly sipped on his whiskey. He'd discovered an interesting connection between the way he drank and the emotions that alcohol suppressed in his grief-stricken mind.

'I could never have guessed,' Kostya squeezed out. 'I saw

you with Yoko before that. You were walking in the park, and I was driving by. I was so happy to know you were doing fine, even without me,' he said, turning to look at the spot where the dog had found its final resting place.

'I understand… and understand me, please! I couldn't call you… I just couldn't. I know you loved Yoko. I saw it every time we went for a walk. You probably wouldn't understand what happened to me after that,' Sasha said, placing his glass on the table.

'Believe me, I'll try,' Kostya replied with a sad smile.

Alexander reached for his glass again and gulped down its contents.

'I don't know how to describe it in words,' Sasha said honestly.

'Emptiness?'

'Yes… exactly. But that scourge doesn't come alone. I didn't want to talk to or see anybody; I didn't want to live. I lost the will to live. I drank heavily as hell every day. I don't even remember how many times I was drunk driving. Understand, I didn't just disappear for you; I ceased to exist for everyone. It was horrible. How many times did I drink myself to sleep at night only to have the same dream where I failed to save her life?'

Alexander poured whiskey into his glass, and taking the bottle, Konstantin did the same.

'I thought a lot: why do I need anything material if it becomes so useless at the very moment when someone's life depends on that? It's all vain and meaningless. Besides, I'd got used to the fact that Yoko would wait for me in the hallway whilst I washed, got dressed and ready to go out with her. For her, I was her whole life. Do you understand? Me! Yoko always forgave me; she didn't know how to get offended, betray, gossip, conceal or cheat… and what did I do? I couldn't even save her. I didn't even want to hear the words of the vet that it was "impossible."'

Sasha stopped and stared in the distance. He was trying to get a grip on his thoughts and chase away the overwhelming emotions.

'I'm afraid to ask, but how did your mum and dad react?' Kostya enquired, hiding his eyes.

'Dad was fairly reserved, at least when I saw him. But we're very much alike, and I'm sure he was crying at night, just like I was. But in the morning, he just came out of the bedroom as if nothing had happened. And mum…'

Another glass of whiskey was sunk.

'Mum was worried,' Sasha continued. 'Of course, Yoko had become another child to her who she had to spoon-feed at first, raise and love.

'And I was drinking and drinking and drinking. To tell the truth, brother, I thought I would drink myself to death. And then, at some point as if something clicked in my head, I tried to assess the situation soberly. I sat down. I had a smoke and started thinking. Dad was unhappy, though he never showed it. Mum was wandering around the house aimlessly, always upset and ready to cry at any moment. And I - what should I say? I was heartily sick of everything. And that leash… I couldn't look at it without tears welling in my swollen eyes.

'I was sitting like that, assessing everything, and I decided it was time. I got into my car and drove around the cold city, stopping only for a breather and to have a smoke. Then, I don't know why, when I stopped yet another time, there was a house in front of me with a brown roof. I'd come to the breeder. At first, I didn't have the guts to press the buzzer — you know? I felt uneasy. But then I did it. She was, of course, surprised, though she recognised me.

'I went inside, and we sat down. I told her the entire story. Of course, she cried, and then she asked: "Why did you come here?" I was silent. I was silent for five minutes. She understood everything and said: "I have one girl now. We called her Aiko. Would you like to look at her?"

'I wanted… I wanted that most than anything! We entered the room. It was weird to be in that house again. I was so naïve. I thought when I came for Yoko it was the first and the last time… I was so wrong.

'The girl was agile and so cute. I asked Nastya: "What does Aiko mean in Japanese?" She lowered her eyes at first, then she raised them at me and said: "Child of Love."'

'You had no choice but to take her,' Kostya said, smiling. 'She's so cute. I didn't know Yoko when she was her age, but I can see that Aiko is completely different. And something tells me you love her even more.'

'Of course,' Sasha replied calmly. 'How can I not love her? She's such a mischievous child. She doesn't listen to anyone, and she shows her temper. It's true, she's quite the opposite to Yoko.'

'Have you started comparing her to Yoko already?' Konstantin asked.

'Of course; I can't help it. My life, my dear friend, is split in two now. Can you see that?'

'I'd call it "Life before," "In the loyal eyes of a friend," and "Life after."'

'That's right. It's just like that.'

Kostya thought about how weird life could be. Having witnessed several deaths in his lifetime, he'd segmented his life into 'Before,' 'During,' and 'After.'

He was sad. He wanted to howl like a wolf! Only he could not; they weren't animals, but human beings. Though how much humanity was there left in them?

Up until that moment, the people – that crowd from his dream – were absolutely devoid of emotion; they lived solely with the purpose of earning money and obtaining fame. He'd thought the same thing about Sasha, who was sitting there next to him at that moment pouring his soul out.

"There is hope," Kostya thought. "We still have something bright in us. It makes us move on but remember those who, unfortunately, will never be with us again."

'And what's with Ilona?' Konstantin asked carefully upon returning from his ruminations.

'And what's with Ilona?' Alexander imitated him. 'Nothing has changed, absolutely nothing.'

'Have you seen each other?'

'Yes,' Sasha said nonchalantly.

'Will you tell me?'

'For God's sake, if only there was anything to tell!'

'Does she know?'

'No.'

'Did you see each other before the accident?'

'No. After.'

'And you didn't tell her?'

'Why would I?'

'That's true.'

Sasha lay back on the foldable chair and gazed up at the stars.

'Let's say,' he continued, 'I saw what I expected to see.'

'And what did you expect to see?'

'Everything looked sad, my friend. I already told you I know everything that's going on in her life.'

'And?'

'Nothing special. We met. Actually, I ran into Ilona near the house. She was surprised, naturally. I suggested we talk, and she agreed. Then she started lying, saying everything was excellent in her life, that things were getting better and better, that she liked her work and was getting paid much more than before. The last part was a peculiar bone to pick with me; I thought it was unreasonable. I knew that every word was a bald-faced lie straight to my face, as if I was just a fool!

'We went to some place to have some coffee, and then we went back to her house. She asked me never to appear in her life again. I didn't answer, I just waved my hand and left.'

'Did you see anything in Ilona's eyes that could make her get back with you?'

'That's the trouble – I didn't. I'm not ready, and I'm not actually in a hurry; I have enough time. I think more about Aiko, a little less about Yoko, and only then about Ilona and other things.'

Not taking life as a given — that's what Konstantin thought about on his way back home after his conversation with Sasha. He got to the second floor, quietly opened the entrance door, and silently slinked in.

Kostya wasn't drunk. The bottle of whiskey the two of them shared had not influenced him in any way. The only thing he wanted to do was to get into bed. The thoughts that haunted his mind were far from joyful, rather drearily definite, and so rueful one could simply give up everything, lie down and die.

We will never forgive ourselves. Never. Such a gift is given only to shallow people. Each of us understands deep in his heart that he shouldn't have been rude to his mother and argued in vain with his father to prove he was right, which at first seems so necessary, but then just turns into ashes.

Konstantin was lying in bed but couldn't fall asleep. Nerves. Work. Plans for the future that didn't seem so carefree anymore. Everything was over. He naively believed such ruminations were the result of the sad news he'd received a few hours earlier. Ah, if only that were the truth, at least for a while. Lying to yourself is like stepping into the abyss in an endless search for the meaning of life, which boils down to not dying today but tomorrow, while hoping that tomorrow will never come.

Evening walks became a habit once again. How could one refuse to spend time with a four-legged friend who, with her small steps, brought a glimmer of light into the gloom that had so tactlessly penetrated every corner of Konstantin's inner world? And the source of this light? That Aiko would be loyal to Sasha until the end of her days, however long or short it turned out to be.

Arriving home, Sasha tiptoed into his parents' bedroom, where Aiko was lying and snuffling. He exhaled. Everything was alright – he could go to bed now. But just like Kostya, he couldn't fall asleep for a long time.

Sasha was reliving the last day of Yoko's life. He looked at his hands, and for a second it seemed that his arms were elbow-deep in blood. Shaking and focusing his eyes, Sasha calmed down: his hands were clean. But his conscience? Hardly. The day would never come when a man who has lost his truest friend would forget about the moment right before the very end.

'Hi! Well, how are you, rascal?' Sasha asked, stretching out his hand that was free of the leash.

'Fine, just working. Today we had a meeting with the investors from China. We sat for a long time and discussed a lot of things. There's a chance that my project will be approved.'

'That's great! I won't congratulate you yet as it's too early, but I'm glad things are looking up for you.'

'Yeah, it's probably good; I don't know,' Kostya replied, at a loss.

Aiko, who was growing very fast, ran beside them, jumping and trying to lick Kostya from head to toe, and only then continue their evening ritual.

'Aren't you happy?' Alexander asked in surprise. 'I thought getting backing for your project was the thing you've been striving for, isn't it?'

'Yeah, of course,' Kostya said hastily, 'but I have mixed feelings. On the one hand, I can hope for a promotion, a bigger salary and all that stuff, but on the other hand, success would mean I'd have to leave, and I don't know how long for.'

'So, what's the problem?'

'I'd have to leave my family.'

'And?'

Kostya fell silent. How could he explain to Sasha that for every success in life, you have to pay something?

'I worry about my loved ones,' he squeezed out from himself.

'Believe me, everything is gonna be alright. They'll be okay without you.'

'Yeah, I know; but I don't want them to be okay without me.'

A month passed. Kostya, Sasha and Aiko were spending a few hours a day together, and it felt like it would be like that forever. Their conversations distracted them from the weather outside. They didn't need much else. They could discuss practically anything, remaining unshakeable, faithful, and what looked like old friends.

One such evening after their walk, Kostya wanted to have a drink. After all, he'd won the tender and his project had been approved by the investors.

'Sash, to celebrate my humble victory, so to say, I'm thinking about having a drink today. What do you say?'

'What are we drinking?' Alexander perked up instantly.

'Wine - I'll get a couple of bottles from home.'

'Wine?' Sasha winced slightly; 'maybe something stronger?'

'No. Today, the right to choose the drink is mine. Where shall we sit? Maybe in the "Finland", or at Zhenya's place?'

'Oh, thanks a lot; I don't want that!' Sasha said, laughing. 'Do we need snacks?'

'Not really. And it doesn't matter to me where we go.'

'Yep, me neither,' Alexander agreed. 'Let's do the following: we'll have a walk with Aiko; I'll take her home, and then…' he paused. 'Though wait, why should I take her home? Okay, I've got it. Tell me: can I go in your car with her?'

Aiko was running around the perfectly manicured lawn near Sasha's house, while he and Kostya were setting the table and chairs and preparing to sit and drink the homemade wine. Alexander sat down first and started opening the bottle, whilst Konstantin was enthusiastically watched the dog scampering in completely unpredictable directions.

'Sash, open the tap for her,' Kostya said, without taking his eyes off Aiko. 'She'll be thirsty after running so much.'

'Will do,' Alexander responded.

With the preparations finally complete, both young men laid back in their chairs with their glasses filled with wine.

'Here's to your success, Kostya,' Sasha toasted.

'Sorry, but no; we'll drink the first one without clinking glasses.

'To Yoko,' Sasha uttered quietly.

Kostya nodded in response and emptied the first glass of wine for that night in one go. Alexander turned around, looked at the place where Yoko was buried for a few seconds, and drank his wine.

'And now,' Kostya began, pouring more drink into their glasses, 'now to my success.'

They drank. The wine was amazing. Even Sasha, who drank wine very rarely, noted its fascinating taste.

'Hey, listen, I completely forgot — what's going on with your Tamara? Are you in touch with her?'

'Don't you have anything else to ask about?' Kostya responded with a vexed expression on his face. 'No, we don't communicate. What's the point?'

'You should see her, my friend.'

'Why would I do that? What for?'

'So you can understand whether you need it or not.'

'You think this approach would be productive?'

'There's no better way. How much time has passed – a year, two years? Well, that's enough. You've changed — don't even try to deny it! It's more than likely she'll have realised a few things for herself. You have too. Believe me, the feelings which bother you at inopportune moments are familiar to me, too. I think about the same things,' Sasha said, and took a sip of wine. 'Just out of interest, text her. You'll chat easily, you'll see. The main thing will be what happens after you see each other.'

'And what, in your opinion, should happen?'

'Nothing special, unfortunately, at least, judging by what I felt after my rendezvous with Ilona.'

'And what did you feel?'

'It's still too early to say. I need to wait.'

'I think, in my case, it's still too early, too.'

'You won't know until you see her.'

'Who knows?' Kostya responded wistfully. 'I want to believe that every person we meet in our life is meant to be met along the way. Everything is interconnected, and it may not be obvious, but the logic behind what happens can only be defined after the event. You may say I'm exaggerating or giving these ruminations too much meaning, and you might be right. However, these thoughts never leave me.'

Sasha didn't respond. An expression appeared on his face that spoke eloquently of the reminisces that were overwhelming him in that moment.

'No,' he said after a pause. 'I won't say you're not right. I'll tell you how I met Ilona.

'It happened two years before she came to work at my store. I was probably eighteen or nineteen at the time; it doesn't matter. I was going on some business, driving through the little park. I stopped at the traffic lights and saw her crossing the road. Ilona looked so attractive and unapproachable; I thought back then: "it'd be nice if such a girl chose me." I was an ordinary student then, albeit the son of well-to-do parents. But I hadn't amounted to much myself, then.

Time passed, and I started dating Regina. Den and I opened the clothing store. Our business was going beyond great. And then, one ordinary working day, our senior manager brought me a pile of résumés. And whose CV do you think I saw in that pile? Ilona's!

'I called her for in an interview and she came. Can you imagine, Kostya? She came to my office… two years later. I could've only dreamt about that! Of course, I hired her on the spot. And then you know everything. I've told you a hundred times.'

'Does that mean you also believe the visualisation of goals isn't nonsense after all?'

'Of course.'

'For the first time in my life, someone doesn't look at me like I'm an idiot after saying those words,' Kostya said, smiling.

'Well,' Sasha got up from his chair, 'everyone has a right to their opinion.'

They were standing in front of Yoko's little grave. Aiko started barking.

'What's with her?'

'She sees,' Sasha said calmly, exhaling thick clouds of smoke.

'Yoko…'

'Yeah. It's said that dogs see our world in black and white, but, indisputably, they can perceive much more than us.'

'Of course. It's only they – our four-legged friends, however irritated or angry we are, can forgive us everything and keep loving us every day,' Kostya said, and shivers ran down his spine.

'I'm sure that none of the girls or women could ever look at me with eyes full of love and trust. They all want something. Each of them has their own vested interest.'

'You changed the subject somewhat roughly,' Sasha said in surprise. 'Yeah, they're like that, I agree. But is it all bad? I mean, you understand it. Yeah, they want money and to live better than before they met you. It's normal.'

'But isn't that a bit mercenary?'

'Even so, let it be. You know what to expect from them, and that means nobody can hurt you. Sure, disappointment is possible, but only if you expect something from the girl. So, just don't expect anything! Act as you think you need to. In any case, everything you're ready to do for her, you'll do for yourself first. Why? That's simple. Those emotions we receive seeing the joy in the eyes of a significant other are incomparable with anything else. And about your idea that none of the girls would accept you as you are — you're wrong. You're still too young, Kostya, to be so disappointed in people.'

'Does it depend on age?'

'No… but the older you get, the fewer new people you allow into your world.'

'Are you sure about that?'

'Well, why do you need them? You reach your goals,

become fulfilled as a person, and the main thing – there are so many criteria for selection which become more difficult to meet with every passing year.'

'I should've got married at eighteen or twenty,' Kostya said. 'I was dumb and inexperienced. I blindly believed in love. I had a passion for love. I thought it would always be like that. But no; the environment changes. We grow up and become more thoughtful and taciturn. We won't get drawn into useless bickering again…'

'And we leave,' Sasha continued his train of thought, 'quietly, and without saying goodbye. There aren't many people I'd like to bring back into my life. I get you, Kostya.'

'It's impossible to bring them back,' Konstantin answered sadly. 'It's a crazy idea.'

'You think so?'

'I know it for sure!'

'Please explain.'

'They change as we do and usually become worse. Those negative attributes I was trying to put up with only intensify, and whereas before I could quite easily ignore those obvious flaws, now my eye is already trained upon them. I'd rather return to the person I was a few years earlier, the one who was joyful, reckless, and not laden with the baggage of that knowledge. I used to make choices without understanding where they'd lead, but now I know.'

'There are always exceptions to the rule,' Sasha remarked.

'Still, I'd rather return to certain situations when I felt happy.'

'What about the people who were the reason for that happiness?'

'No... or just for a short while. The past is dead, Sasha, and we don't need it. We learn to live with our current circumstances. It's the worst, but it's necessary.'

'Would you want Toma back?'

'You ask difficult questions, Alexander Anatolyevich,' Konstantin said, curling his lips. 'More no than yes.'

'Even I know why,' Sasha blurted out sarcastically.

'Come on then, read my mind,' Kostya said, and laughed.

'Why would I read it? Don't I have enough mental tomes of my own? Logic, my friend, logic is the main thing. You don't want her back because you already know her, her habits and her behaviour. Did you ever have moments when Toma pissed you off? Of course, you have. You're not stupid enough to think that wouldn't happen again, the same manipulations.'

'They wouldn't work,' Konstantin said firmly.

'Exactly. And why's that? Because you've learnt to live without the woman without whom you once couldn't even imagine your future.'

'Well, then,' Kostya asked quietly, 'do you really think I should text Toma?'

'Why not? You have the advantage of surprise here, so use it. You have absolutely nothing to lose, so it's worth a try. Who knows, maybe everything will work out for you. So, yes, text her. I'm sure you haven't forgotten her number.'

'Of course, I haven't; though I don't understand why I still remember it.'

'Text her, Kostya. Relieve yourself of these doubts. And, by the way, regarding other girls – don't worry about that. You'll leave soon, and the whole world will open up for you! There'll be so many there, you'll find the one.'

'It's weird to hear that from you, Alexander. Why haven't you done the same thing?' Konstantin asked, trying to peer into his friend's eyes.

'Well, because I've already found her,' Sasha replied sadly. 'Only she doesn't understand that. She keeps trying to prove something to me. And for what? I loved her the way she was. I didn't propose? Bullshit! She wasn't sure about me. That's what the problem was. I didn't deserve that either because of my actions or my words.'

'You have Aiko,' Kostya noted quietly. 'She's worth more than any of that crowd of dolled-up lasses. How did you even find the strength to go there again and sign up for the same terms? It must've been painful for sure.'

'I didn't have a choice. What would I have turned into if I hadn't brought Aiko home? A drunkard. I couldn't go on like that. The hardest part, Kostya, is when you don't have a reason to get up in the morning; when you don't see the point of going out or speaking to anyone. Just like Yoko in her time, Aiko didn't let me die in the dark abyss of mental torment.

'It only seems that a dog depends on its owner. He feeds it, gives it water and takes care of it, it's true. It's these furry naïve creatures who save us every single day, however, when the injustice of this world threaten to overwhelm us.

'Do you think Aiko can't live without me? That she stands with her front paws on the windowsill and keeps looking for me in the distance? No! That's nonsense, lies, bullshit. It's me, Kostya; I'm the one who wakes up every morning and runs home from work in the evening knowing that there, in my apartment, someone is loyally waiting for me. It's impossible to buy something like that... you can't force a person to do it; they'd fail somewhere along the way. But not them.'

'Because they don't know how,' Konstantin said, and sighed. 'Take care of Aiko, Sasha. Take care of her as well as you can, because you mean the world to each other, whereas I'm still alone.'

Almost half a year passed.

Konstantin went through passport control and finally emerged from the airport and into Tashkent.

"I'm back," he thought, exhilarated.

He soon spotted Camilla joyfully waving at him in the crowd of meeters-and-greeters. They chatted near her car for probably ninety minutes, and only after that did Kostya return to his apartment.

It was New Year's Eve, but the phone remained silent. Sasha wasn't even going to call. Kostya, who was used to his friend's disappearances, didn't expect anything and was sitting at the festive table so elaborately prepared by his family. He was planning on going to Camilla's place, but a little later, after the clock had struck midnight.

Holiday greetings were coming from everywhere: partners from China, acquaintances from Sweden, Poland, Turkey, England, Argentina, and France; everyone was sending some simple but kind words that drew feelings of gratitude in response.

The phone rang.

'Hey, Happy New Year!' Kostya heard.

'Hi, and Happy New Year to you, too,' he replied.

'Am I imagining it, or are you really back?' Sasha asked.

'I'm back.'

'Why didn't you call?'

'Why would I? Aren't you interested in how I'm doing?'

'Hey, stop that crap! What's your plans for tonight?'

'With the family now, and then I'm going to Camilla's place.'

'And what's there?'

'We'll have a drink and chat. Join us if you want.'

'Oh, I'm celebrating with Zhenya at my father's cottage. Maybe you should join us?'

'No, I already promised her. Sorry.'

'When are you going to Camilla's place?'

'I'm about to leave. If you want, we can meet up for a little while.'

'Let's do that.'

'I'll call you when I'm there.'

Having arrived at Sasha's house, Konstantin got out of the car and leant on its roof. As usual, a familiar figure with a leash in his hand appeared from the entrance. Aiko seemed even happier to see him than her owner, jumping and wiggling when Kostya tried to stroke her. She even tried to bite him and yelped now and then. It seemed as if Aiko, the child of love, was scolding Konstantin for such a long separation.

'So, how are you doing?' Sasha asked when Aiko had finally had enough of playing with Kostya.

'Everything's fine, thanks. How are you? What's new with you?'

'What new can there be? Everything's the same. Aiko's growing, as you may see. But her temper… dynamite!'

'She's just true to her nature, unlike people,' Kostya commented.

'Right.'

They stood like that for about twenty minutes and exchanged the usual small talk until it was time to say goodbye.

Konstantin understood that it was likely to be their last encounter, and so it was. At two in the morning on the first of January, these two people who were more connected than even they could imagine separated forever.

Alexander went home so he could go on celebrating the holiday with Zhenya later, and Konstantin went to see Camilla before leaving his hometown soon after.

But no matter where he was, no matter whom he met, again and again Kostya searched in the crowd for that loyal look in his friend's devoted eyes, which was imprinted forever in his memory, and remains with him to this day.

Konstantin Alekseyevich put the book aside and prepared to light a freshly rolled cigarette.

'Now I get it, dad,' his daughter said, wiping away her tears.

She looked at her old man tenderly.

'Now I understand why you stubbornly refused my wish to get a dog for so long. Did you really never see each other again?'

Konstantin shook his head in response.

'But she wasn't your dog, was she? Why do you still remember her?'

'Because a friend, Mila, a real and devoted friend will never leave your thoughts just because you stopped seeing each other for a million reasons.'

He lit the cigarette.

'She was my friend and remained so even after leaving for the other world. How long has it been?'

And for the first time, he allowed himself to cry.

Andrey Grodzinskiy